The Vicar Man

Amelia Crowley

To Kate and to Kt without whom this book would never have happened

The Place: a small island just off the British Coast

The Year: 1740

No, wait: 1813

Um…

1696?

Actually…

Look.

There's almost certainly a king, very possibly named George.

1

It was a dark and stormy night.

Well of course it was: bright, sunny nights are pretty rare on the Island, whatever might happen elsewhere, and the weather there is usually damp and frequently over-dramatic. So nobody was paying much attention to the climate when the Inn door rattled open, admitting a great howl of wind and rain, and with it a tall traveller clad in a billowing, rain-darkened greatcoat.

As he took off the enveloping garment and shook the water from its copious folds, a sudden hush fell, only to be immediately swallowed in a babble of conscientiously idle conversation.

I looked at him across the crowded room and I thought: "Oh bugger."

It's not that I don't like strangers: I don't really have much of an opinion about them one way or another. It's just that strangers almost never come to the Island -a fact that speaks for the good taste and discernment of strangers everywhere- so when I considered the sudden presence of *this* stranger, a week before the vernal equinox, following a catastrophically bad harvest the year before.

Well, as I said: bugger.

Looking around the room I saw that most of the patrons were

eyeing him with a sort of sullen covetousness that he probably took for insular suspicion. Old Man Morris, though, wore instead the sort of expression that the Poet would probably have described as Native Guile, which is to say that he looked as though he knew something we didn't know and was desperately wishing somebody would notice.

I poured a pint pot of ale and headed in his direction.

"Don't often have visitors in these parts," I observed companionably.

"That we don't," he agreed, reaching a withered hand for the mug on my tray.

I shifted, leaning casually against the wall and, incidentally, moving the tray just out of reach: "A body might wonder what he was here for."

"That they might."

He assumed what was probably meant to be a look of deep cunning, but only succeeded in looking sulky and short-sighted.

I moved the tray out of reach again.

"Perhaps a body might tell a body, if'n his throat weren't parched an' dry fra' setting' so long by the fire wi'out e'en a drop o' ale."

"Look," I abandoned the game; "Do you know what he's doing here or not? Because if you don't want to tell me then I'm sure there's someone who does and this tray is ruddy heavy." He looked at me reproachfully: knowing something I didn't was probably the most fun he'd had all year.

"Well, hand it down then lass, and mebbe as I'll ha' summat to tell ee."

I sighed and relinquished his prize: "Fine, but can we drop the Rural Cunning routine? I've been on my feet all day dealing drinks, and I've no time to listen to the full performance right now."

"Fair enough," he took a long pull of his pint; "What I heard is Billy Suggs and young Davey Mullins took a boat to the mainland a couple weeks back, an' let it be known as how there's been no church nor chapel on the Island since the last Reverend died, and we here is all living like sinners, just longing for some good shepherd to come an' lead us back to the fold. Saw the Bishop himself, they did, an' laid it on nice an' thick, an' now here's this fine fellow come to save us all from perdition."

He twinkled at me like someone's wretched old grandad, and I felt my heart sink into my boots.

"So he's for the fire, then?"

"That he is," the old man smiled; "a fine offering he'll make, the God will be fed, an' we'll see a good harvest this year, you mark my words."

I rallied slightly: "He might not be eligible."

"Don't you worry none," he patted my hand reassuringly; "the boys had a good look round an' talked to them mainland folks an' to the Bishop, an' they said as how that one lives all alone in their big old vicarage, with naught but a manservant, an' spends his days doing of good works in the congregation. He said it was a shame, the Bishop did, an' a terrible worry, for a man like that ought to have hisself a wife, to keep his house in order, an' see to his comforts an' such.

Well, the boys said as yes that was a shame but never mind: we've plenty o' pretty girls here to choose from!" And he leered at me, in a companionable sort of way.

"So don't you worry, Dora-lass," he repeated; "that one's plenty eligible, you mark my words."

I looked back across the taproom to where the stranger now sat, hunched awkwardly over a table with the look of one already regretting his choices in life -or perhaps that was just sea-sickness from the journey. He was tall, and gangling, with surprisingly bright eyes behind small round lenses, a sharply pointed nose, and a fluff of blond hair that stood out on his head in all directions. He looked like nothing so much as an attenuated parrot.

As I watched, Molly sauntered over from the other end of the bar to give him a pint and an unrestricted view of her bosom. He startled as though he had been kicked, jarring the table and slopping ale all over himself and the understandably irritated Molly, who sauntered off again in a huff.

I could see the old man's point.

Look: every place has its own oddities and traditions. Maybe there's a bridge you can only cross with your eyes closed, or a well that gets decorated with flowers once a year, or it's terribly unlucky to say the word "beetle". Old customs that have survived through the years and make the community what it is. The Island Faith is just like that, only a lot more bloodthirsty.

The origins of the Island God are shrouded in mystery, but wherever he came from, he's been here a long while. You see him everywhere: carved into hearths and lintels, moulded onto mugs, worked in embroidery, even painted on the sign for the Inn if only I could get the thing clean enough to make out.

The God is tall and skeletal, with twisted antlers, knife-like fingers, and a maw full of needle sharp teeth. Or that's how he looks in all the pictures anyway. And most of the time, that's all there is: just a lot of creepy artwork.

Well, a lot of creepy artwork and one long-held belief: sacrificing a virgin to the God will ensure a good harvest.

In theory, of course, the virgin ought to be one of our own. We are all, after all, devout worshippers of the God, who would each be overjoyed to have the honour of serving as sacrifice and thus replenishing our Island's pitiful wealth. In reality, though, being burned alive on a wind-wracked headland in tribute to something that looks like a peculiarly vicious toast rack is - well, all I'll say is it's not most people's first choice in life.

So people find excuses: they marry young and start churning out babies, thus disqualifying themselves in the most important regard or they just go out fishing and stay gone until the coast is clear: "So sorry, it was the tides, see?" or; "I got caught on a sandbar" or in one memorable case; "I drowned." Failing that they insist that they are simply not worthy of so great an honour, and kick up such a fuss on the way to the bonfire that they have to be let go.

The sacrifice has to come willingly to the flames, you see.

The last person who came close to being burned was my mother.

She wasn't born on the Island: she washed ashore one November as a wet and skinny eighteen-year-old waif, sitting on a raft beside a massive box of books. She refused to say where either she or the books had come from so, since no-one was likely to come looking for her, she was quietly marked down for the next year's sacrifice and sent to live with my Dad and Gammer over the winter.

Now Dad was a gentle sort of lad, and not much inclined to shelter someone all Winter only to betray them in the spring, so as soon as he found the opportunity he took her aside and quietly explained what was probably in store for her. And was promptly belted around the head with a large, heavy, and if it weren't so waterlogged probably very expensive copy of De Naturis Philosophae (1st ed.).

Well what would you do if some young man took you into his house then told you you'd have to do away with your virginity or perish?

Still, despite this unfortunate beginning, by the time May Eve rolled around the question was very clearly moot. And thus I, who made my first appearance on our benighted isle some four months later, can fairly claim to have been disappointing everyone since before I was born.

My mother died in childbirth, whereupon everyone made a tremendous fuss about the Punishment That Awaits Those Who Would Rob Our Master, while cheerfully ignoring both our frankly terrifying childbed mortality statistics and the fact that they themselves had done everything in their power to disqualify themselves as soon as possible.

I was mostly raised by my Gammer, who despite all evidence to the contrary considers herself the Island's wise woman; by the big box of books, which taught me to use words like "childbed mortality statistics"; and by my Dad, an increasingly distant figure who as the years went by spent more and more time out at sea all alone. Not because he was mourning his lost love, mind, but because he was a lousy fisherman at the best of times, and round here it's never the best of times.

He died in the end, but not of a broken heart. It was a turbot.

Anyway, one way or another, the Island hasn't actually seen a sacrifice since before my Gammer was born.

I disqualified myself as soon as I reasonably could.

It wasn't exactly difficult: one night I got hold of a couple of jugs of ale and got Davey Mullins - him with the fishing boat - nicely sozzled. One tipsy walk into a field later and he was soon flat on his face and snoring, only to wake up with a terrible headache, and your humble servant rolling over beside him asking whether it was as good for him as it was for me.

I still feel a little guilty about that sometimes.

Mind you, it did the job well enough: Davey went bragging to all of his friends, just as I knew he would, and his friends told their friends, and all the other girls looked side-eyed at me and whispered behind their hands the way I knew *they* would, and a couple of months later he did the exact same thing in rather more authentic detail with someone else, and that was more or less an end to it.

So maybe I'm not technically disqualified, but I might just as well be.

I sometimes think virginity is just a social construct anyway.

People give you funny looks if you say things like that around here.

Either way I was, as far as anyone else was concerned, firmly off the menu for the forthcoming celebration, and it looked very much as though our innocent, psittacine visitor was on it.

I really ought to do something about that.

The question was, what exactly ought I to do? I gazed vaguely around the crowded room in the hope that some sort of inspiration might strike. It didn't.

I tried gazing at the reverend stranger instead, which merely depressed me.

It wasn't as if he was the first visitor to our shores, not by a long shot, it was just that most people who came here either weren't qualified for the position, or else took one look at the place and were gone again before anyone could so much as get the kindling in.

The last long term visitor we'd had was the Poet.

He'd taken a room in the Inn for the whole of the last summer, which had got people very excited, especially when he turned out to be the romantic sort, prone to rhapsodising over our "rough, primal" lives, striking tragic attitudes, and wandering the cliffs during thunderstorms, getting soaked to the skin.

You'd think that sort of behaviour would be enough to give even the most determined girl a headache.

So everyone was very disappointed when he told Molly in *strictest confidence* that his current rustication was due to his having inflamed the affections of no less than three noble women of impeccable pedigree, causing one of them to break off a highly advantageous engagement, and destroying another's marriage to a charmingly monied, military gentleman who had been away for some time and who was, though amiably dim, entirely capable of counting to nine.

It was not, he confided, these damsels who troubled him. Nor was it the swarm of male relatives who had borne down upon him with pistols and small swords, demanding satisfaction. It was the third lady.

She, a timid and delicate creature, had found herself completely overcome with adoration for his romantic person. To such an extent that when he attempted to withdraw quietly from town for the good of his health, she followed him, declaring her intentions to abandon her family, throw off the constraints of respectable society, and follow him, her only love, wherever he should go.

Naturally the poor boy fled.

And so it was that he washed up on our appealingly desolate shores where, he hoped, no fragile elfin beauty would dare to tread.

Of course everyone was terribly disappointed by this tale.

There was some suggestion that perhaps he had, if not completely invented it, then at least embroidered the truth a little, but any hope that he might be up to snuff after all was dashed when Molly mentioned just exactly where he had told her his story. Which was in Molly's bed.

And then he told Annie.

And Sal.

And young Jessie Taylor who should have known better.

So that put paid to that idea.

At the end of the summer he left, saying that he was off to the Mediterranean to do "something truly revolutionary", still glancing over his shoulder for fear of his devoted sweetheart, and leaving a trail of broken hearts from one end of the Island to the other.

I considered our visitor. Could his moist and unassuming breast conceal a heart filled with forbidden passions? It seemed dismally unlikely.

So, as I said, bugger.

2

I squinted at the dear soon to be departed once again: could I fool him the way I had Davey Mullins?

He didn't exactly look the sort to bandy a girl's name and reputation about, particularly a girl he'd only just met. Still, looks could be deceptive and, in the end, what had I got to lose? At any rate I could hope he'd be too decent to outright deny any claims that I might make on the subject. I picked up the jug and headed over to refill his cup.

Which was still half full.

The other half, I suspected, was currently adorning Molly's overworked bodice and his own equally damp but rather less curvaceous chest.

Nothing daunted, I hefted the jug and went to top it up anyway.

His hand shot out to cover the cup.

Not, alas, in time to keep me from pouring.

The dark brown stream splashed merrily over his hand, spattering the tabletop and further moistening his already dampened cuff. I retracted the jug.

"Oh I do beg your pardon, Sir!" I improvised wildly; "Let me fetch you a cup of our finest, as an apology for the accident."

Our finest ale is very fine indeed, but it is also unexpectedly strong.

He winced: "No, thank you, that really won't be necessary."

"Why, I can't go soaking your good shirt and just walk away without a word," I blithely ignored the fact that Molly had done the exact same thing not ten minutes earlier; "it wouldn't be seemly, Sir."

"Really, I - I assure you, it's quite alright."

"At least let me replace this one."

"No, really," he lowered his voice as though sharing a dark and terrible secret; "I don't much care for ale."

"A cup of wine then."

"No, that's..." he stopped, struck, "Do you *have* wine here?"

"Certainly we do: the innkeeper makes it himself. Out of grapes. And things."

"Things?"

"Things, sir."

"Ah," he shifted awkwardly, "that sounds, um, that sounds lovely I'm sure."

"I'll just get your wine then, sir, and I'll be back in a trice."

"Ah, no!" He caught at my apron strings as I turned to go.

"Sir?"

"No wine, sorry"

Well, it was his loss: Tom's wine might not be quite as astonishingly good as his beer, but given the difficulty of finding anything remotely grape-like on an island as cold, damp and grey as ours, it was well nigh miraculous all the same. Still, I decided not to press the matter.

"But there must be something I can get for you?"

"No!"

"No Sir?"

He fidgeted uncomfortably, though whether out of embarrassment or because of the ale seeping into his smallclothes I wasn't sure.

"The truth is," he lowered his voice once more; "The truth is, I don't really care for alcohol at all."

I blinked at him: on the Island it was generally understood that a good dollop of alcohol was all that stood between us and a miserable fluxy death via water borne diseases.

Perhaps I had misheard: "You don't care for alcohol, Sir?"

"No."

"But what do you *drink*?" I was so flustered I forgot the "Sir".

"Water mostly."

"Water?"

"Yes, or watered wine if I must. Small beer if there's nothing else to be had."

I wasn't entirely sure what "small beer" was. Beer, on the Island, meant anything from a thin brownish water deemed suitable for children and pregnant women, and a potent glistening brew which, in the words of the Poet "Creeps up as softly as a kitten, and kicks like a brewer's dray."

Perhaps if I put it in a very small cup? I turned toward the bar again only to be arrested, once more, by my apron strings.

"*Water.*" He gave the word a quite unnecessary emphasis; "Please."

I fetched him his water. And a cloth for the spill.

Well, this clearly wasn't going to be as simple as getting the man drunk and then thanking him for a delightful evening, so what now?

I couldn't simply tell him what was in store: he would most likely decide I was delusional. In which case it was entirely possible that he would go looking for some suitable, responsible person in whom to confide the terrible secret of the barmaid's madness. And that would bode very ill for your humble correspondent.

Even if he didn't go spreading the tale of poor, mad Dora far and wide, it was unlikely that he'd want to pay much more attention to a woman who claimed his unassumingly pious flock were planning to truss him up and roast him as a picnic lunch for a clawed monstrosity from beyond the veil.

Well when you put it like that it does sound a little unlikely, I admit.

So what were my options?

I could actually disqualify him, I supposed.

It wasn't that I was entirely repulsed by the whole...*physicality*... thing, it was just that it all seemed rather pointless and undignified. Even on an island as small and damp as ours I could find any number of pursuits more appealing than heaving about under another sweaty body. Scrubbing out the old beer barrels, perhaps. Still, I thought I could do it, if push came to shove.

Which, as I understood it, was how these things usually took place.

The sticking point in all this was my prospective partner. He was, admittedly, not the most attractive specimen to grace our squelching shores, but that wasn't where the difficulty lay. No. The problem, not to put too fine a point on it, lay with me.

The Poet, bless him, once called me "A sloe eyed beauty whose tempestuous curls tumble over her bounteous abundance" which is a nice way of saying I'm a plumpish girl, whose hair frizzes when it rains. Which is always.

My eyes aren't half bad, it's true, but even allowing that I'm not the most hideous creature on Earth, I didn't have much faith in my abilities as a seductress: I'd never wanted to do it before, I didn't really want to do it now, and I hadn't the faintest idea how you were supposed to go about it.

So what else was there?

I could try to make him as uncomfortable as possible and see if I could drive him off the Island that way. Uncomfortable was more or less the Island's natural state anyway, so it shouldn't be too difficult.

On the other hand, since his arrival less than an hour ago he had been subjected to the unnervingly covetous stares of the entire complement of the taproom, been drenched not once but twice in Tom's third best brown ale, and struggled through my obtuse attempts to get him drunk, and he showed no sign of budging whatsoever.

In addition to which he drank water and apparently wasn't dead yet.

All of which suggested a personality far to stubborn to be driven off by mere discomfort.

As I stood lost in thought, my eye caught on the figure of the Island God carved over the door, his clawed hands outstretched, jaws yawning open as though to engulf any who came within his reach. His eyes, gouged crudely out of the wood, had darkened over the centuries, becoming two bleak, hollow pits, seeming to offer nothing but agony and despair. Staring into them I began to have the faint sense of something, just out of reach. Something distant and foreboding, and beyond that a fragile hint of...

"Are you quite alright?"

I broke off from my reverie abruptly.

"What? - I mean, whatever do you mean, Sir?"

"Only you've been standing there for almost half an hour"

A prickle ran up my spine: "Do you mean to tell me, Sir, that I've been standing here, all unknowing for half an hour, transfixed by that cruel image over the door?"

"What?" He looked where I was pointing. "No, no, I mean that you brought me my water and then you just stood there, looking vacant".

By "looking vacant" he of course meant "searching desperately for some way to save me from your bloodthirsty nearest and dearest", but I couldn't exactly tell him that. I quirked an interrogative eyebrow at him and attempted to look forbidding. He shifted under my eye: "I wondered if you were quite well."

"Mind you," he rallied somewhat; "I wouldn't have been surprised if you had been hypnotised by that thing." He gestured at the God: "Creepy, isn't it?"

"I suppose so." I squinted back at the carving. Yes, it was, in point of fact, very creepy. But I was an Islander and knew what it meant: I was *allowed* to think it was horrible. Visitors should have more manners.

"I've never really thought about it before, Sir. We have them all over the Island. I could show you some time, if you liked."*And perhaps you might catch just the tiniest hint of what's in store. If you aren't literally too oblivious to live.*

"All over the island you say? How, ah, how odd. All those bones and antlers and things. I wonder what it's for?"

"It's traditional, Sir." I said, suppressively.

"Oh, is it? Sorry. No offence meant of course".

I wondered how he intended to reclaim for the Lord the faithless heathen of our septic isle *without* offending against our ancient and abhorrent traditions.

"Still," he confided; "It gives me the willies."

"Does it, Sir?"

Now there was an idea.

In order to follow out the plan that was now busily fomenting in my mind, I first needed to know exactly where my quarry was staying.

So it was that, while remaining outwardly calm and courteous, I secretly observed our reverend guest and, as the Inn closed its shutters for the night, slipped like a shadow into the greater gloom without and flitted phantom fashion in his wake.

Which is to say that I waited till closing and followed him home.

I am not, it must be said, built for stealth. My tread is far from cat-like, and my aforementioned abundance reflects any glimmer of light like a pair of infant moons. Still, I knew all the dips and corners in which a body might lose herself, and my cloak, being not of midnight black but a serviceable brown, blended well with the murky stone, umber mists, and general mud of my surroundings. So I made decent progress, hanging back but keeping him in sight.

He seemed a little twitchy, turning several times to look back the way he had come, and on one occasion necessitating a sudden plunge into a nearby ditch, but eventually his feet turned off the path I'd expected him to take and stopped, not at some neat row of cottages but at the Rectory.

If the word "Rectory" sounds impressive I should warn you straight away that it isn't.

The Rectory looks exactly like all the other houses on the Island: a small, thatched structure, shaped a little like a loaf of bread and built from rough stones that are whitewashed every year, yet still manage to maintain a patina of greyish brown.

Inside I knew there would be a single long room with a fireplace at one end, a scullery in the corner, and perhaps half a wall to screen the sleeping quarters from prying eyes. Outside, beyond the kind of low, stone wall that's more an invitation to trip over than any kind of barrier, were a few stunted trees, a tangle of briars, a bindweed-covered well, and the brooding ruin of the old church.

This edifice, which had sent the Poet into paroxysms of delight, stood towering over every building in sight -which was admittedly no very difficult feat- and looking perpetually in imminent danger of collapse. It gave the impression of having been ruined in some terrible tragedy, but in fact had been only half built by the time the mastermind behind its construction had been hauled off by my esteemed ancestors and turned into friar fricassee. They'd set fire to the church too, after, but it hadn't burned very well, due to the damp.

The whole prospect was damp, chilly and inhospitable, feeling eerily isolated despite the fact that the nearest neighbours were only at the end of the lane, and showed glints of companionable warmth through their shuttered windows.

In short: it was perfect.

I stood for some time, contemplating the scene, imagining the horrors that might - with a little encouragement - lurk behind every shadow.

"Ho there!"

Of course, in doing this I had forgotten to lurk myself.

I pulled my wits together and prepared to put a brave face on it.

"Give you good evening, Sir."

"Oh," he seemed rather surprised that I answered him; "it's...I don't think I caught your name, actually. From, ah, from the inn, um, yes?"

"Dora, Sir. From the Inn, Sir, yes. Barmaid."

"Oh, ah, Norman. Norman Poltwhistle. Reverend. *The* Reverend, that is."

He pulled himself together: "The Reverend Norman Poltwhistle at your service ma'am."

"At yours too, I'm sure Sir."

These commonplaces seemed to soothe his nerves somewhat: "Do you, ah, do you often take walks down lonely country lanes in the middle of the night, Dora?"

"Yes, Sir," I lied.

"Really? It seems," his hand described a dissatisfied arc;

"unusual."

"I don't have time during the day Sir. Too busy."

"You aren't, ah, nervous at all? In such a desolate place, I mean?"

I fixed him with my sternest expression: "*Should* I be, Sir?"

He recoiled beautifully: "No! Of, of course not! I just meant with the..." again he waved uncertainly; "the...the trees, and the darkness, and..."

I took pity on him: "It seems perfectly normal to me Sir."

"It does?" his bright eyes stared at me. "You don't feel a sense of all-encompassing dread, at all? No chill fingers of horror creeping down your spine?"

Well, now that he came to mention it, perhaps I shouldn't be so sure of myself. "Oh, but of course I'm used to it, Sir. I suppose to one such as yourself, coming from the mainland, such a solitary place might be a little unnerving."

"It might?"

For some reason, being told that actually, perhaps the place was rather creepy seemed to have settled his nerves a little. I soldiered on, nevertheless.

"Indeed it might, Sir. And of course the way the wind howls like the souls of the damned, and the shadows seem to watch you as you pass" I blessed the Poet, wherever he might be; "and there's the sense always of something following you, just out of sight, wherever you may go, well, I suppose that could be disconcerting to someone who wasn't used to it." I gave him my biggest, cheeriest smile: "But that's all quite usual to me Sir."

"All, quite...usual?"

"Oh, yes Sir, and of course I don't believe anything they say about the ghost of Anna Matilda."

"The...ghost of Anna Matilda." I was beginning to wonder if he really was a parrot.

"Oh *yes*, Sir, she walks the Island they *say*, Sir, whispering and catching at your clothes, and overturning furniture, but I never pay such stories any mind."

"You don't?"

"Oh, no Sir, it's all nonsense I'm sure.

Oh, they say the spirits of drowned sailors walk our shores, and the ghosts of those who've died untimely walk our streets, and poor Anna Matilda walks these hills searching for the man who killed her, but that's just fireside tales, Sir.

Of course I'm not saying no-one ever saw anything: very likely there was something peculiar once, and the rest of the tale came from there, but it won't have been anything real. Just a cat, or a sheet blown by the wind, perhaps, and someone saw it and got carried away. Why, I'd swear that if you were to ask anyone in these parts, anyone at all, they'd tell you there wasn't a single ghost on the Island." This at least was true; "You being a visitor, Sir, and them wanting to make a good impression."

He looked greatly relieved at these words. I couldn't have that.

"So you don't believe a word of it?"

"Not one word, Sir.

Of course," I assumed an expression of deepest concern; "you probably shouldn't go walking after dark, Sir. Not being used to it. Just in case".

Relief fled.

"But there, Sir, I've kept you talking for far too long, and you not used to our damp nights either. You get inside Sir, where it's warm"

"Ah, yes, of course, I'll just, ah, goodnight then miss."

"Goodnight Sir."

And he sped down the path like a rabbit before a fox.

I let him get almost to his door before adding: "Don't forget to lock up now, Sir."

None of the houses on the Island have doors that lock.

It was very late when I got back to the Inn and the room I shared with Molly, and later yet before I could blow out the light, but when at last I could settle down to sleep it was in a warm glow of self-satisfaction. I had a plan, and it was coming together beautifully.

If the Island gave him the willies, then willies he should have.

3

The next morning dawned blearily, or perhaps that was just me.

I had spent what remained of the previous night engaged in furtive handicrafts, and while sleep, came, when it did come, as the well-earned reward of dutiful endeavour, it also came at about twenty minutes to cock crow.

And how that bloody cock crowed.

I staggered out of bed, swore at the aforementioned cock and dragged on a clean shift and stockings still half asleep. By the time I was fastening my skirts I was more or less conscious, but my fingers fumbled clumsily at my laces, finally producing a knot that I could not, in my current state, unpick, and which I feared would have to be cut.

Abandoning the fight, I pinned my curls into a semblance of order, made my way down the narrow, crooked stairs, and set about putting the Inn to rights.

Given that it was only middling-sized and without more than basic furniture or any decoration beyond a few gruesome carvings here and there, it should have been difficult for our taproom to ever become more than mildly disordered. And yet, every evening the good people of the Island rose to this challenge.

I collected cups and pint pots from the tables, windowsills and mantlepiece, righted a few upturned benches, and had the place halfway back into order again before I had so much as spared a thought for Tom, the innkeeper, whose nightly duty this theoretically was.

I wasn't surprised to find him absent, mind.

Tom's family had been innkeepers since time immemorial, every one of them a friend to every person ever to cross their threshold. When his parents died everyone had expected him to carry on running the Inn, bandying words with the patrons, and generally making himself the life and soul of the party. He did his best, for duty's sake, to live up to these expectations, and he hated every moment of it.

He didn't like crowds, or loud noises, or having half a dozen people all trying to talk to him at once. He didn't even enjoy talking to one person, if it wasn't a person he particularly liked or a subject he liked to talk about. He didn't get the jokes people made, seemingly at random, or like the sudden way they all laughed, out of nowhere, at things that weren't even slightly funny. Still he pushed on, miserably, for almost a year, shrinking all the time under the need to be loud, friendly and larger than life.

Then, one blustery night a few months after I came to work there, Himself With All The Apple Trees came sweeping into the Inn and fixed his eyes upon Tom's with a hypnotic stare.

He had been trying the hypnotic stare on everyone he met, and it hadn't had much effect so far, but Tom, who never liked eye contact at the best of times, had quailed and turned away under the force of those ferociously staring eyes. Encouraged by this, Himself stared harder, shuffling around to maintain eye contact. Tom pulled back, retreating behind the bar, and Himself followed, drawing himself up magisterially and probably already trying to decide which hypnotic command he should first try on the clearly mesmerised Tom. Who, finding himself with nowhere left to retreat, chose this moment to abandon the niceties and thump Himself squarely on the shins with the tapping mallet we keep under the bar top.

Well, accidents will happen, and the back-of-bar area is *for staff only*.

After that, Tom decided there were better ways to honour his family legacy than by making himself miserable every night, and he let me and Molly take over the day-to-day running of the Inn. For his own part he retreated to the brewing sheds, where he spends his days creating every kind of ale under the sun, and a few that should only exist in the realm of blissful hyperbole. Our patrons, for their part, down them all with complete indifference to fragrance, colour, flavour, or whether the label on the barrel reads "Stout", "Pale Ale" or for that matter, "Turpentine"

A lesser man might have grown dejected in the face of this unrelenting enthusiasm, but Tom has never faltered in his dedication to his art.

He loves it. He's happier than he could ever have been trying to live his parent's lives, and the ale he brews is phenomenal.

Even so, from that day on Himself never had another beer in our Inn that wasn't somehow flat, shorted, or tinged with mysterious sediment.

From the slop bucket if necessary.

I had rolled up my sleeves and was just making a start on scrubbing the floor when the Inn door banged open and Molly staggered in.

How do I explain Molly?

Try this: imagine the most beautiful woman in the world.

Not the most beautiful woman you've ever seen: the most beautiful woman in the world.

Take your time.

Let your mind form every limb, trace every lock of hair, set every light in her perfect eyes, sing with the echoes of her mellifluous voice.

Then, once you have every aspect of this unparalleled beauty firmly in mind, imagine her wonderful face contorted in rage as her companion ignores her in favour of the even prettier girl who has just walked into the room. The incandescent beauty accidentally stealing the first woman's escort is Molly.

Fortunately she is as good-hearted as she is lovely, or she wouldn't have a friend left on the Island.

Not that Molly did anything much to encourage her admirers. Nothing more than any other barmaid would, anyway. She's a warm hearted, friendly girl, who was never happier than when she was in the throes of a new romance, and never more despairing than when said romance inevitably fell apart. Quite often on the morning after it started.

There wasn't much I could do about it: Molly was always so sure, so certain that this time, this time was different, this was it: the one, true, perfect love that she had been waiting for. And then, well.

Two months earlier she had been desperately, blazingly in love with John Anders, until he threw her over for Grace Perry. Then, heartbroken and swearing never to love again she sought refuge in the arms of Mark Liddell, who cherished and adored her and taught her to believe in love once more, then dumped her in favour of Bessie Corran. From Mark she went to Lettie who ditched her for George then ditched George too. *He* naturally turned to Molly to find mutual consolation for their shared woe but, just as the colour was returning to her pretty cheeks, and the light of love beginning once more to kindle in her eyes, he reconciled with Lettie and dropped Moll like a rotten egg. And so it continued, as predictable as it was heartbreaking: she would come in, her face aglow with happiness, to tell me all about her newest romance, and I would smile and say all the right things, watching her build her tower of dreams, while inside I was wondering, all the time, just how long it would be before the tower collapsed and her hopes were once more trampled underfoot.

It appeared that the latest trampling had arrived a little ahead of my prediction.

Molly was not at her best: her hair was half unpinned, her skirt hitched past her knee, and her bodice barely holding itself together, yet despite this brave show of normality I could see that all was not well. I stood, knuckling my back, and arched an enquiring eyebrow.

Molly, taking this as her cue, paused in her wobbling progress and turned her reddened eyes in my direction.

"Jimmy Bettan," she declared in her sweet, musical voice; "is a bastard."

Sensing that she had more to say on this subject I remained silent and was rewarded for my patience with a series of increasingly emphatic pronouncements concerning the exact nature of Master Bettan's bastardry and what, exactly, Molly wished him to do with his bastard promises. Once the tide of denunciation seemed to be ebbing away, I ventured to ask exactly where she had spent the night, if not in the arms of the bastard Jimmy Bettan.

She blinked her liquid - if slightly bloodshot - eyes at me.

"Well of course I was with Jimmy: I wasn't going to walk back here in the middle of the night, on my own now, was I?"

I, having done precisely that, offered no answer. I don't think she expected one anyway.

"But!" she added, flailing one hand for emphasis; "He'd better not think I'm going to do that again!" Here followed several more interesting revelations on the personal habits of James Bettan Esquire. The bastard.

Eventually even Molly had to run out of steam. As she stood there, shaking minutely, my heart was wrung. She looked miserable, overwrought, and even tireder than I felt. I knew, improbable as it might now seem, that she had honestly loved the bastard Jimmy.

I pressed one tragic shoulder in what I hoped was a consoling fashion.

"Why don't you go and lie down, Moll? I can finish up here by myself, and you know the place will be all but dead until evening"

Her lip trembled: "Are you sure Dora?"

"Of course I'm sure," I offered her a bracing smile; "You go and get a few hours sleep and everything will soon look better, you'll see."

"Well, if you really don't mind." She turned towards the stairs with wobbling step then abruptly turned back; "And I'll take the afternoon."

"You needn't bother." In truth I quite liked having the bar to myself: it was quiet, and no one bothered me.

"Yes I will, Dora." She was so uncharacteristically firm that I didn't know how to argue. I made the attempt anyway and found a dainty finger pressed suddenly to my lips.

"Yes I *will*, you needn't think I haven't noticed."

I attempted to ask what exactly she had noticed and was flatly shushed.

"Your laces are in a knot," well, yes they were; "your shift's on backwards," was it? "And you look nearly as tired as I am."

I drew breath to defend myself against these foul verities but she rolled straight over me: "You've got a sweetheart, haven't you?"

I stopped, stunned. This particular interpretation had completely passed me by.

Molly took my silence for assent: "There, I knew it! I'll bet you hadn't been home half an hour before I got in, and here you are trying to do all my work as well as your own. Well I won't have it. You let me have the afternoon, and you go and see your sweetheart." She smiled mistily: "You should have a sweetheart, Dora. You deserve one." With this she turned again and tottered towards the stairs. "Unless," she added; "it's Jimmy Bettan."

And with a final murmur of "Bastard" she was gone.

The day passed as quietly as I had expected: a few people came in about noon for mugs of ale, the cockerel strutted in through the open door and had to be chased out with a broom, and I stole a few minutes to have a word with Tom about the accounts, but apart from that I was free to scheme in blissful solitude.

The sun was slanting long shadows across the floor and I was dreaming of a triumphantly vicarless Island by the time Molly came yawning down, her hair attractively disarrayed and her bodice freshly straining across her chest.

According to Hints To Young Ladies Approaching Their First Season (1ˢᵗ ed), these Cheap And Tawdry Tricks should have terribly diminished Molly's charms, giving preference to those damsels who took Pains to Cultivate An Air Of Mystery. It was a testament to her incomparable beauty that they didn't. It was probably just as well that she *didn't* attempt an air of mystery, in fact, as if what the book said was true, then I doubt the Island's collective constitution could have borne it.

More to the point she was looking much better and I was glad to see it.

"Oh, Dora, I overslept!" She looked at me in honest contrition: "I did mean to give you the whole afternoon to yourself, I swear I did!"

Since I hadn't expected to see her till evening I was able to assure her that I wasn't at all upset and, indeed, was only grateful that she was affording me this few hours respite. She looked unconvinced and, strangely, the more firmly I reassured her the less willing she seemed to believe me, continuing to beg my pardon until I was almost shouting soothing placatory nonsense over her barrage of apologies. Before my calming words could reach a crescendo that would have rattled the cups on their shelves and brought Tom running, panic-stricken from the brewing sheds, I caught myself, took hold of her hands, looked her firmly in the eyes and, as quietly as I could manage it said: "It's alright Molly, really it is".

That seemed to work. I've no idea why, for it was exactly what I'd been saying for the last twenty minutes. Still, having appeased her at last I didn't dare enquire further lest I set off another round of self-recrimination. Before she could change her mind I gave her hand a heartening pat and, free at last, darted out to the safety of the Inn yard. Once out of range of further apologies I collected the fruits of my midnight labours, then set off down the hill to the Rectory.

I kept a careful watch as I approached the house: it wouldn't do to have Reverend Poltwhistle discover me there, especially when I'd been so insistent last night that I had no free time during the day. By good fortune though, when I arrived I found both house and garden empty.

I undid my bundle and set to work.

I daren't linger too long about the house: I might be able to excuse my presence in his garden, but inside his home was another matter. So I couldn't do as much as I should have liked, but I overturned a few pieces of furniture, moved some candlesticks around, and hid his box of tallow dips under the rather lumpy pillow.

When I was done you couldn't have sworn the place was haunted, but you wouldn't have been entirely sure that it wasn't, either. That accomplished I turned my attentions to the garden.

I confess I enjoyed myself there.

From the trees I hung several little figures composed of sticks and string. I had been at some pains, the night before, to ensure that every one of these looked not *quite* right. Legs dangled oddly. Heads sat like pimples on shoulders far too broad, or threatened to overbalance bodies much too small. Arms either swung beneath their feet, or were omitted entirely. Taken as a whole, they were beautifully disconcerting. I poked several more into the briars and, as an afterthought, balanced one on the lintel of his door.

The door itself I scratched with a bodkin, until I had created the impression of clawed fingers, scraping at the wood. I scratched around the windows too, in as threatening a manner as I could manage, then breathed on several of the little squares of glass, and scrawled my fingers jaggedly down the fogged glass.

Finally, to the longest overhanging branch I could find, I tied a noose.

It was all wonderfully artistic.

The scene completed, I headed back up the path a little way, tucked the rest of my bundle out of sight under a fallen tree, and hurried the rest of the way back to the Inn.

I had to scramble somewhat to make myself presentable before the night's first customers should arrive. A fact that only cemented in Molly's head the idea that I had a secret lover somewhere about. I had no time to disillusion her on this, however, as she was busy serving ale, charming our customers, and being conspicuously absent whenever Jimmy Bettan attempted to catch her eye - no easy task in a taproom as crowded as ours.

For my part I poured ale, rebuffed the customers, served Master Bettan with what I hoped was an expression of grim forbearance, cleaned tables, and kept a weather eye out for the good Reverend Poltwhistle.

He arrived, as soggy as ever, and took what I suspected would have become his customary seat, if he weren't going to be turned into a burnt offering before the week was up. I offered ale, which he predictably declined, but after some back and forth he consented to try a particularly weak, unassuming specimen of Tom's brewing. He thanked me for this profusely, then sniffed dubiously at the thin, straw coloured liquid, before sipping cautiously and allowing his face to fall into the appearance of mild discomfort which I suspected was as close as he dared get to an actual expression of pleasure.

At least he didn't turn it down altogether this time. Why, at this rate I could probably have him nicely insensible by the end of the year. Since the end of the year was a good nine months too late, though, it was just as well that my plans no longer hinged on getting the poor man rolling drunk.

Thinking about these plans, I risked another glance at the Reverend.

He didn't look much like a man haunted by beings from beyond the veil, I had to admit. He looked damp, for the most part, and rather dejected.

The Poet would have said that his was the look of a man languishing in thoughts of his long lost love, but the Poet was like that, and nothing anybody could do seemed to change him. In the case of the Reverend Norman Poltwhistle, I suspected that his was the look of a man languishing in chronic indigestion.

Still, I consoled myself, perhaps he'd been out all day, ministering to his flock. With a little luck he'd return home, find his house in a state of discomfiting confusion, and pass an uncomfortable night before waking to the sight of my gruesome creations in all their grisly glory. Buoyed by this thought, I discharged the rest of the night's duties with my customary vigour, pausing only to sneak occasional glances at his reverence from behind the pewter pots.

By the end of the night he seemed, if anything, more miserable than he had been at the start. He had made several attempts to join the cheerful gossip at other tables, but they all fell ominously silent at his approach, and not all of Molly's rallying banter could seem to raise his spirits. Rather the reverse, in fact: he twitched spasmodically whenever she came near, as if anticipating another shower of ale. When closing rolled around, he unfolded himself from the table, gave an awkward nod to nobody in particular, and shuffled self-consciously out.

Before the door had finished closing, every table in the house erupted into furious conversation. It was possible, I reflected, that the sheer force of his unwelcome would be enough to drive the Reverend Poltwhistle off in search of kinder shores.

Best not to count on it though.

* * *

I could see that the lateness of the hour would not prevent our patrons from dissecting every inch of the Reverend's actions since entering the Inn that night. Admittedly those actions amounted to little more than "Sat down, bought a drink, failed to talk to anyone, went home" but it was clear from the hubbub that filled the room that sitting down and not really doing much was now somehow the most exciting, most controversial activity since Millicent Sherry sold the same cow to three different buyers. And it wasn't even her cow in the first place. Getting any sort of gossip out of the Reverend's meagre doings might have struck me as getting blood from a stone, but the crowd had taken a good hard grip and were prepared to keep squeezing.

Well I didn't have time for that nonsense: I had somewhere to be. I took a deep breath, surveyed the vibrant, convivial scene, and prepared to make a nuisance of myself.

I bustled about the place, collecting tankards whether their holders were finished with them or not, wiping tables out from under elbow-propped chins, screeching benches back into place over the hush of intense conversations, and generally doing my best to project an aura of disagreeably virtuous industry. In the face of such diligence even our most devoted topers lost their enthusiasm for their art, and by the time I began noisily heaving out the mop and a bucket of water the last of our guests was already tottering out of the door.

I paused in the act of swabbing down the floor: Molly was staring at me in as much horror as though I were a mirror and she were developing a spot.

I smiled weakly.

She managed, with one vague, limp-wristed gesture to convey the sentence "What in the name of the darkest hell do you think you're doing, why have you driven all our customers away, and is it possible, my dearest friend, that you have finally lost your mind?"

I tried the smile again: "It saves time for the morning?"

This time the gesture said: "Oh, Cannibal Lord, she's finally lost it! Now what am I to do? I'm not supposed to handle this sort of thing: Dora was always the sensible one and now she has taken leave of her senses. I think I feel one of my headaches coming on."

Molly's actions always spoke more eloquently than her actual speech did.

I sought refuge in bald-faced inference: "Look, Moll, it's late and I've got places I'd like to be," true; "and I might not want to get up too early in the morning," also true; "so I thought, well, what's the harm with getting a little bit of a hurry on, just this once?"

This last was entirely untrue: I had known exactly what the harm would be and, had, in fact, been counting on it.

At my words, however, Molly's face lit up like a threepenny candle.

"Oh, of course, Dor, I completely understand: you just get on with it then."

She dithered hazily between the stairs and her sense of duty.

I decided to take pity on her: "Why don't you head to bed, Moll?" In a flash of sudden inspiration I added; "There's no need to wait up for me: I don't know what time I'll be in."

At this Molly beamed, and with the most knowing look ever to grace her beautiful face, she leaned over and patted me on the cheek. This mark of approbation delivered she drifted happily up the stairs, pausing only briefly to call down: "Don't do anything I wouldn't do!"

I wondered what in the world that might entail. Recreating the experiments of Paracelcus, perhaps?

Shaking off the haze of contemplation, I ditched the mop, snatched up a shawl to cover my hair and shoulders and, thus armoured, set off into the night.

The walk back to where I had left my bundle was a chilly one, but otherwise without incident and, after a brief panic while I ascertained that everything was, in fact, exactly where I had left it -no *this* gnarled fallen tree, by *this* ancient mossy stone- I quickly made myself ready.

Making myself ready meant, in this case, powdering my face and arms heavily with flour, outlining my eyes with a scrap of charcoal, swathing myself tastefully in a couple of sheets in imitation of a winding cloth, and unpinning my hair which, unruly at the best of times, responded to the damp night air by twisting itself gleefully into a bedraggled mass of twining tendrils. This done, I pulled my shawl back over my head and crept breathlessly up to the Reverend's doorstep. At the rectory all was dark, quiet and still.

The perfect setting for a haunting.

I paused for a moment, not quite believing that I was really going to attempt this. It seemed suddenly irresistibly ridiculous that I, in an attempt to save an innocent, if rather tedious, man from the murderous machinations of my fellow heathen Islanders, should wrap myself up in the clean bedlinen and whisper ghostly imprecations under his door.

I shook myself: time to take this seriously. I took a breath.

"Murrrrrderrrrr-" I broke off, consumed with giggles.

Another breath.

This time the giggling overtook me before I could even begin to speak.

I pressed a fist against my mouth to smother the sound, and almost choked on a handful of flour. As I spluttered desperately to control myself, I heard a movement from within. He'd heard me!

But what had he heard?

Perhaps I could still redeem the situation if - another fit of giggling burst forth, pealing in the chill silence of the night like so many merry bells chiming all at once. I scrabbled away in a panic and darted around the corner. Just in time, for the door creaked open and a pale flicker of candlelight illuminated the birdlike discomfiture of Reverend Norman Poltwhistle.

I held my breath, terrified all at once into silence. Whatever had possessed me to attempt this? How could I possibly believe my disguise would work? What in the world was I going to say if he caught me?

Oh, hello Reverend, it's a nice night for a walk. Why yes I always dress up like this when I go for a stroll: it's all the rage these days, didn't you know? Somehow I doubted even he would believe that.

The door creaked shut again.

I exhaled all at once, then caught my breath again as if he were about to leap out on me from some shadowy corner.

He didn't, of course.

Slowly, heart pounding like my head after one of Tom's more experimental brews, I crept up to the door again. It stood closed, silent and still, but a thin line of yellow light glimmered from the grimy windows: the Reverend had not yet gone to bed.

I contemplated going back to my own bed: it would be warm, dry, moderately comfortable and, best of all, not occupied by a mainlander parson who popped up out of doorways when by rights he should be shaking in his sheets.

A mainlander parson who would soon be frazzled to a crisp if I didn't find some way to get him off the damn Island.

Well, drat.

Time to try again.

Properly sombre now I took a moment to compose myself, knelt down to the crack under the door, and opened my mouth to scare him silly.

My mind went blank.

I could not think of a single thing to say. All my carefully planned accusations, threats, cryptic utterances and other Things To Terrify Hapless Vicars With had fled my mind as swiftly as if they'd just heard they were to be the guests of honour at the next sacrificial barbecue.

Perhaps a deathly moan?

I prepared to chill him to the bone.

And instantly got the giggles again.

I leapt back around the corner as if the wild hunt and all its hounds were on my heels, and the door banged open in my wake. For a while I just huddled against the rough stone wall, afraid to breathe.

From the doorway came the distinctive silence of a man listening with all his might.

Finally he muttered something, the door grumbled shut once more, and my heart slowed its thundering to a mere gallop. I crouched to creep away, then stopped myself: unless I was very much mistaken, what he had muttered had been "Jumping at shadows."

Did he mean me? Could he *see* me somehow? Or, was it possible that my inept cackling had managed to achieve the desired effect after all?

Well, if disembodied giggling would serve to frighten him, I should just have to giggle until he ran distracted. I knelt back down, put my lips to the crack of the door, prepared to giggle and...nothing happened.

I tried again.

No giggle.

I took a breath, screwed up my courage, and tried to force a laugh out of myself.

Nothing doing.

I sat down on the step, still in my sheet, and contemplated the sheer absurdity of my existence.

Even that didn't raise a titter.

Inside the house the light went out. The Reverend was returning to his bed. Time for action Dora. *Say* something! From nowhere, the words of the Cuckoo Song came into my head.

Out of sheer idiotic desperation I pressed my lips to the crack and in my reedy, tuneless voice sang: "Sumer is icumen in…"

The effect was immediate.

As I dashed round the corner again, I heard the crash of a man bolting incontinently out of bed. The door slammed open, and Reverend Poltwhistle stood panting on his doorstep.

I waited till he had gone back inside, gave him five minutes to calm down, then carried on where I'd left off.

We made it through the whole song, piece by piece. After a while he took to sitting with his back to the door, but I could see where his shadow cut out the light, so I crept round the house and sang under his bedroom window instead. By the time I reached the last "Sing cuckoo!" I had led him from pillar to post and back again, and had no need at all to force the giggles that fell from my lips.

Having done my worst, I peeled quietly away from the window and, under the cover of my shawl, tiptoed back to the road.

Once safely hidden behind the fallen tree, I paused to consider the situation. I could go home now and account it a night well spent, or, perhaps, I could push things a little further…I stood up and looked toward the rectory.

The Reverend's pale face stared out at me.

No going back now. Crossing everything that could practically be crossed, I assumed the expression of a woman betrayed. It was, to be precise, the expression of Molly in the middle of her tirade against the bastard Jimmy, but there was no way he could know that.

I raised an accusatory finger and pointed at his fluffy blond head.

He stared back.

I wrung my hands and mimed an agony of despair.

He pressed an eye against the grubby window pane.

I mimed harder.

He moved towards the door.

And I ducked behind the tree again.

I wondered whether he would come out to investigate further, but, after a decent interval, the door creaked shut again and I resumed my tragic gesticulation.

We spent about an hour in this way, with him scurrying between window and door, and me popping up and down like a peculiarly indecisive rabbit. Eventually though the Reverend's candle died down, and his door stopped swinging open, so at last I followed his example and headed home to bed.

Scrubbing myself clean under the pump in the yard I considered the night's work.

It was, I thought, not bad at all. I could make up some nicely malicious folklore to explain all the giggling and singing, and poor Anna Matilda seemed to have made a pretty firm impression.

Yes, I decided, as I crept past Molly's musically snoring form and clambered, muddy sheets and all, into bed: that had all gone rather well.

4

I rose the next morning in the brightest of moods

It's true that I'd caught only a few hours sleep before the benighted cock began his caterwauling down below, but nothing, not even the discovery of a trail of muddy footprints right down the stairs and out to the courtyard, could dampen my spirits.

I sighed contentedly through my yawns.

I smiled as I tucked up my petticoats to scrub the floor.

I winked at my ghostly reflection in the greasy surface of the slop-bucket, and hummed to myself as I lugged it out of doors.

I glowed as I tucked an errant curl back into place, remembering the way my hair had cascaded, wild and uncontrolled over my ghastly livid form the night before.

I felt incredible: powerful in a way I had never felt before, as though the world was mine for the taking. I was a terrifying creature of the shadow realms and I revelled in it.

I danced back through the door, bucket swinging merrily, twirling through a roomful of imagined grotesques, head singing with my triumph, dizzy with success. And ran slap into Molly as she came downstairs.

* * *

"Oh, lord, sorry Moll'." I fought the smile off my face and tried to show proper concern for her bruised toes and, oh dear, grease spotted petticoats.

But Molly was smiling too, a wistful, indulgent sort of smile that I'd never seen her wear before.

"Don't you worry a bit, Dor'" she beamed, apparently oblivious to any injury; "it's good to see you properly happy for once."

Since I was fairly sure Molly didn't imagine twirling into people while wielding imperfectly cleaned slop-buckets was the usual way that one expressed joy I was unsure what she meant by this. Was I usually so very dismal? Or was I just *im*properly happy? And what did Molly know about impropriety anyway?

Apart from everything the mean-spirited part of my mind put in.

"Besides," she added, taking me by the shoulder and turning me to face the taproom; "You've got a visitor. Looks like your admirer can't bear to be parted from you".

I followed her pointing hand. Reverend Norman Poltwhistle was standing in the doorway. Suddenly it was very easy to stop smiling.

I shot back around the doorframe with a speed that, had he seen me, would undoubtedly have put the Reverend in mind of a certain spectre the night before. "What's he doing here?"

Molly looked puzzled: "Don't you know? I thought he was here for you!" Her perfect forehead creased in thought. "Is he bothering you? "Cos I thought he was your sweetheart but if he's not I'll..."

I caught her arm before she could do something appalling like demanding to know the Reverend's intentions: "No! He is! I mean, he isn't my sweetheart, but he is the man who isn't my sweetheart, if you understand."

"I don't."

I glanced round the doorframe again: Reverend Poltwhistle was still standing, waiting patiently. Either he hadn't noticed us, or he was being remarkably polite. From what I'd seen so far, it could be either one.

I lowered my voice further, just in case: "He isn't my sweetheart," Molly's face fell; "but he is the reason I wanted to get away last night." Now she looked merely puzzled. "He's supposed to be being sacrificed at the end of the week, and I don't want that to happen so..."

Light dawned: "So you're trying to disqualify him!"

No, I'm trying to scare him witless so he'll run away and never come back.

No, no time to explain now: even terminally polite vicars could only wait patiently for so long, and like it or not, I needed to know if he'd seen through my disguise.

"Yes. I'm trying to disqualify him." My conscience twinged: "To save his life" I added.

"Oh, Dora!" For some reason her smile was even soppier than before.

"What?"

"It's so romantic!"

"It is?" I blinked at her in confusion.

I owned several romantic novels. My mother's books could be roughly fitted into a few groups: Household Management, Natural Philosophy, Philosophy, History, and Horrible Things- mostly witch trials and grisly murders. There were also several books of Latin poetry, which I translated with the help of the Natural Philosophy books; one in Greek which I decoded by means of the unnatural Philosophy and the Latin poetry; and two whose alphabet was so unfamiliar I didn't know whether I was coming or going.

Once I'd made my way through all of those several times I had looked around for more to read and the Island had, as ever, not provided. So as soon as I had any money of my own, I'd started saving up and sending to the mainland for any books that might be for sale. These were my romances.

None of them remotely resembled our current situation. To begin with, we ought to have been in a bat haunted castle, or a house on a rocky moor, or maybe an interestingly foreign country, not a muddy little island in spitting distance of the mainland. Then the Reverend would need to be a count, or a lord, or at the very least something other than a reverend, and we'd both need to be considerably better looking and someone would have to be plotting against... well, I supposed that was something.

"Because they're...trying to kill him?" I said.

"Yes! And you're going to save him and," her luminous eyes stared seriously into mine; "you do *like* him, Dora, don't you?"

"Yes?" I didn't dislike him at least.

"There! And he likes you, I'm sure of it, so..." having apparently run out of words, Molly settled for hugging herself ferociously, then hugging me, then embarking on a sudden attack of "improvements" to my hair, my cheeks, my laces and my petticoats, before spinning me back around and pushing me precipitously out into the taproom.

At least she took away the slop bucket first.

Yanking my skirts back into a semblance of modesty, I attempted to stroll nonchalantly over to the door. This was hampered firstly by the fact that the floor was still wet, meaning that I had to creep around the edges of the room, clinging to the walls as if I were afraid of falling in, and secondly by a nagging awareness that Molly was lurking around the corner, grinning her precious golden head off at the thought of my "romance". Eventually I made it to the patch of warm light where the door stood open and where, for a wonder, the flagstones beginning to dry.

"What can I do for you Sir?"

The Reverend looked tired, but his eyes were bright and I could swear that he was biting his lip. I would have felt that perhaps he wasn't such a limp rag after all, but since the person he was so firmly not laughing at was me, I felt under no obligation to be charitable.

He cleared his throat a few times, then in a careful semblance of sobriety said: "I was rather hoping that I might break my fast, but I see that you are not yet open for business".

Oh, thank goodness, he wasn't here to uncover me as his ghost. Molly had done quite enough uncovering already, this morning and I didn't think I could stand to have my imposture revealed as well as my cleavage. I leaned on the doorframe, trying to look charmingly carefree and not like someone sagging in relief.

Now I just needed a good opening line: some way to get him talking, then I could subtly steer the conversation onto the subject of ghosts and, hold on. What was that about breakfast? I pushed away all thoughts of phantasms and focused on the question at hand.

We won't be open until noon Sir. We never are."

"Really?" He seemed troubled by this news; "That seems an, an odd way of doing things: Do you not lose, um, quite a lot of business that way?"

"No Sir. On account of most people work in the morning."

"Ah," he shuffled his feet; "of course I realise that my, um, my position does allow me certain, ah, advantages. I should have considered that, well, um, that not everyone has the leisure to simply…" I took pity on him: "Besides, our customers like to stay late. We make more money if we let them linger over their ale by night, and wait to clean up in the morning."

Relief dawned across his face, swiftly followed by discomfort: "I hadn't meant to imply any disrespect. I should, of course, have realised that, um, that your culture and, and traditions may differ from my own, and that I ought not to expect your world to rearrange itself for, um, for my advantage."

I felt my face assume the sort of expression that was usually directed at me.

On the one hand, given that we were a few scant miles from the mainland, his apology struck me as faintly ridiculous. On the other hand: he had no idea.

Since I had no hands left on which to consider how outrageously reasonable his statement therefore felt, I decided we had better abandon that course of enquiry altogether.

"Do come in, Sir, and sit down. We've nothing really prepared, nothing for the Quality, as you might say, but there's porridge on the fire, and honey to put in it."

"Oh, but I can't steal your breakfast." He looked so hopeful as he said this that I put little faith in his meaning it.

"It isn't stealing, Sir, is it? If I give it to you?"

While he was wrestling with this thorny problem I made my way delicately across the slippery flags, dished out four bowls of porridge, set one in front of the Reverend, and added a spoon and the bowl of honeycomb. If said bowl happened to be decorated with a particularly grisly moulding of the Island God devouring his own struggling breakfast, well, that wasn't my fault, now was it?

"Eat that while it's hot now," I admonished like somebody's stereotypical Old Nurse; "and we've yesterday's bread and new ale to follow."

Setting down my own and Molly's bowls, I put the fourth on a tray, added a good dollop of honey, snatched up a spoon and made my way out into the sunlight.

Tom's brewery was a tumbledown assortment of ramshackle sheds and lean-tos held together with twine and optimism. I set my shoulder to the wobbly hinged door and pushed through into the warm, moist, yeast-scented fug within.

Tom was at the back, half slumped over a vat with his elbow brushing last night's stew plate. I checked that he was still breathing, just in case, then eased the half-eaten meal out from under him, and set the porridge down where he'd be able to see it. Duty done, I picked up the plate, abstracted a promising looking jug from the shelf by the door, and gasped gratefully out into the fresh air once more.

By rights I should have stepped into the poultry yard to look for eggs, but the cockerel was patrolling back and forth with a diabolical look in his eye, so I sent a perfunctory kick in his direction instead and nipped back to the Inn before he could express his displeasure with a rather better aimed peck.

I never spent more time in the brewery than I could help, and I'd hurried more that morning than usual, but when I got back I found the Reverend standing outside in the sunshine, his plate and bowl abandoned.

"Leaving us already Sir?" I asked in my best Saucy Barmaid tones.

He shifted uncomfortably on the spot, eyes on his dusty boots.

"I don't, ah, that is to say it isn't..." He was clearly distressed about something, so I smiled encouragingly and motioned for him to continue.

"I...ah, well...that is..." There's nothing like open, friendly encouragement to render an awkward situation downright excruciating.

"Sir?"

His eyes remained fixed on his toes: "It's the other barmaid."

"Molly, Sir?"

"Y-yes, if that's her name, the one with the, um, the eyes and the ah, and the hair and the..." his hands sketched a fairly predictable outline.

"And what has our Molly been doing, Sir?" I cooed over him like a doting grandmother, but my mind was racing: had she tried to seduce him? It wasn't like Molly to poach. Or at least I assumed it wasn't, not really being in a position to know. But he certainly had the stunned look that I associated with some of her less enthusiastic potential suitors.

"She, ah, that is she... Well she.... Um."

He looked as if he might turn and run at any moment. Had Molly somehow succeeded where I had failed? I'd only been gone a few minutes!

"Out with it Sir!" I commanded in bracing tones.

"She keeps *grinning* at me!"

"Grinning?" I wondered if I had misheard.

"Grinning." He confirmed, in a voice the approximate size and volume of a weevil's.

Perplexed, I peered around the doorway into the taproom.

Molly was sitting demurely at the table, gnawing on a heel of bread. She seemed just as usual: her skirts tucked up "to be out of the way", chemise falling artlessly off one perfect shoulder, a few locks of hair drifting softly against her cheek as if to invite the tender brush of a lover's hand. She was a sight to behold, it's true, but no more than usual.

Just then she glanced up, noticed me looking in, and *beamed* at me.

To call it a smile would be to call Scylla and Charybdis, whose furies churned the sea into a rage and drowned a thousand ships "a couple of fish".

The smile was vast, greedy and inescapable. It glowed like a hundred slumbering embers: warm for now, but threatening at any moment to break out and consume everything in its path. It was a smile to shatter the strongest resolve, a smile that demanded everything, a smile that would not be denied.

Molly scented romance. And she was *hungry*.

I blinked several times to break eye contact, then returned the smile as best I could and delicately closed the door. "I see what you mean, Sir."

"I mean," he gestured helplessly; "she isn't doing anything, she just..."

"Quite."

"And I..." he trailed off impotently.

"It's a nice day, Sir," I said, inaccurately; "just the sort of day to enjoy a meal taken out of doors."

"It is?"

"Oh, certainly, what with the birds," I indicated a couple of scraggly herring gulls; "and the fresh sea air and...everything."

What was I doing? What by the God's grisly grey gums was I going on about? I was supposed to be driving the poor man away, not drivelling about the dubious beauties of nature!

"I'll just bring your food out."

I retrieved the breakfast things and we stood for some time in the pale sunshine, munching in strangely companionable silence. It was actually surprisingly pleasant. If you ignored the mud, the vicious look of the gulls, and the general sliminess of everything, then there was something to be said for enjoying good food and good company on a theoretically sunny day.

Well, that would never do.

"And how are you settling in, Sir?"

Was it me or did his smile falter a little? "Oh, very well really, very well." His expression was wonderfully unconvincing: "Really I've nothing to complain about, nothing at all."

"Indeed Sir?" I looked him straight in the eye; "Why that is excellent news, and I am very glad to hear it."

He shifted in the face of my enthusiasm: "Yes, really, I've no cause for complaint."

Well surely I'd given him enough of an opening by now!

I intensified my examination: "But are you sure, Sir? For indeed you seem tired and strangely wan. Did nothing disturb your rest this night? Not a mouse perhaps, or the inclement weather, or" I looked away to spare my blushes and also so that he wouldn't see me trying not to laugh; "our rough Island food: I know it's very plain and coarse, and maybe it wouldn't sit well with a gentleman such as yourself, for it's well known that the gentry have delicate stomachs, Sir."

"No! No, nothing of that sort, I assure you."

"No?" I assumed my most confiding expression: "It's not the privies, is it? Indeed they all behave so when the wind is up and there's nothing to be done about it. You get used to the smells, Sir, in time."

"No it isn't the blessed privies!"

I'd never heard that adjective applied to our frankly unfragrant facilities before. Still, he was a man of the cloth and he could bless what he pleased, I supposed.

More to the point, if he said that *it* wasn't the privies then he had tacitly confessed that there *was* an it for the privies not to be! I congratulated myself on this convoluted conclusion and pressed my advantage.

"It's just..." he wilted miserably under my kindly eye.

This was it!

He was going to tell me all about the mysterious occurrences of the last night, and his ghastly visions of Anna Matilda, and I would tell a few comforting tales to make it all so much worse, and he'd soon be too frightened to spend another minute on that horrid haunted hillside. I should have him off the Island by lunchtime.

I hoped Molly wouldn't be terribly broken hearted when she heard about my failed romance. It was too bad of me, really, getting her hopes up like that. Still, it couldn't be helped: I would just have to break the news to her very gently. I wondered whether I could persuade her to take over egg collection for a couple of weeks, just while I recovered from the shock?

It couldn't hurt to try.

"It's just..."

"Yes Sir?"

"It's...and I know it's silly because I'm not going to be here long anyway, but," wait, what? Did he know he was going to be sacrificed? Was I wasting my time trying rescue a volunteer?

"But I really can't find a single thing I need and of course it will be easy once, um, once my valet arrives, but..."

I had to know more: "Why whatever do you mean, Sir?"

"Mean? Why what should I, ah, that is, I realise it's a little unusual to bring my ah, my valet over for such a short time but really, I'm so disorganised and..." I could believe it: even if I hadn't seen inside his house, if his conversation was any indication of his usual level of organisation he must live in a constant state of terrified confusion.

"No, Sir, what do you mean about such a short time?"

"Ah well, of course one wouldn't usually need a valet for so short a..." What on Earth was the man babbling about? From what I'd read it seemed those people who had servants were in the habit of dragging them along everywhere they went no matter how short the visit. Presumably in case they came across the sort of problem that only a highly trained professional could handle. Like an untied bootlace.

"...and then of course I still have to um, to pay him, and really the cost of livery, not that he actually wears a..."

He was still talking. I took a deep breath, let the words roll over me in a meaningless hubbub, and silently counted to ten. Then did it backwards. From a thousand. In Roman numerals. And then I tried again.

"No, Sir. What I meant was-"

"And really the expense of maintaining two establishments-"

"*Sir!*"

"...and so when you look at it...um, oh, sorry, yes?"

"You said you were only going to be here a short time, Sir. What do you mean by that?"

"Oh, that?"

"Yes, Sir."

"Not-" I have no idea what he was going to say because I didn't risk letting him finish.

"No, Sir."

"Oh, well that's simple."

"Really, Sir?"

"Oh, yes, well I'm just the locum you see."

I knew my Latin wasn't perfect, in fact I sometimes suspected the writers of my books' Latin wasn't perfect either, but: "You're...a *place*, Sir?" Or was it a sort of insect?

"What? Oh, ha, no: place*holder*. I'm just here until a full-time Vicar can be found. That should only take a month or so, my uncle pro- I mean *the Bishop said*. After that I'll be off back to my own little parish." He flushed self-consciously; "They really can't do without me for too long, you know."

Right. I understood now. Everything made sense. Alright, not the Latin, or the weird ramble about the Servant Question, but the rest of it: Here temporarily, not here to be sacrificed, probably still going to die. It was perfectly clear. And he was probably perfectly doomed. Right

"I see, Sir," I pushed the conversation firmly back on - or at least towards - its original track again; "and you were saying something about a problem of some sort?"

His eyes, predictably, aimed themselves at his feet again.

"Sir?"

"It's the children you see."

Had I misheard him somehow? I tried to persuade myself that "children" sounded very similar to "terrible inexplicable apparitions and attendant ghostly phenomena".

I failed.

"The...children, Sir?"

He nodded glumly.

"I wasn't aware that you had any children."

"I haven't." He smiled weakly: "I shouldn't think I ever will. I'm rather terrible with them actually: never know what to say."

The conversation was running away from me again. While I attempted to restore my equilibrium I resorted to meaningless words of comfort.

"That's no great matter." I patted him consolingly: "There are plenty of people who never have children, and plenty who think they won't then do, as well. You've time yet, no matter what you choose."

"No, not my children."

"You don't have any children." I reminded him, still patting.

"Not them!" He insisted, rather incoherently; "Other children, children here!"

I looked around us.

The yard seemed much as usual: small, wet and completely devoid of juveniles.

"Here, Sir?"

"On the island."

Well that made more sense. Only not really.

"What about the children on the Island, Sir?"

"It's just," he gave me a rather wobbly smile; "it seems they're in the habit of playing in my garden."

I was now completely lost. He took my bafflement for encouragement and pressed on.

"Even in my house, it seems, and I quite understand it, after all the place has stood empty for decades but, well, but I really can't have them trampling through the place now, and their toys were all over the place!"

I hadn't seen any toys when I was there earlier. Had I haunted the wrong house?

But I had seen him perfectly clearly, standing in his doorway: there could be no mistaking that silhouette of a half-drowned chicken.

He was still speaking.

"Little dolls and figures made out of sticks. All very rough but they'd obviously tried their hardest. And then there was a swing, having over a branch. It's obviously a regular haunt of theirs."

The word "haunt" rang bitterly in my ears: oh my precious pernicious poppets! *Dolls!*

"And at least one of them had been through the house, for my things were all disordered and I couldn't lay hands on anything I needed..."

Well honestly! I'd only hidden the candles!

"...don't seem to have any proper bedtime: they were up all night singing songs up and down the street."

My lovely, eerie cuckoo-song!

"I saw them, a couple of times, playing in the field."

Now wait just a minute!

I may not be the most ravishing beauty ever to walk this corrupt and fetid earth (that would be Molly) and I may not be the tallest, either, but I could hardly be said to resemble an unspecified number of children. There was that bounteous abundance for one thing.

I forced myself to interrupt: "Really Sir? Are you quite sure?"

He blinked disarmingly at me: "Well, no, not of that last."

"Well then..."

"I'm terribly shortsighted you see, and I hadn't my spectacles" I wondered what use a dramatic presentation would have been to him; "but I certainly saw at least one figure, dressed in white: it must have been one of their nightshirts."

Oh, really! After all my hard work! Bloody God of the Island consume the man!

Or not, rather, because that was the whole point, wasn't it?

I wondered whether I could play it off somehow: big, weepy eyes perhaps, *but Sir, there are no children on this Island,* but he was still talking.

"...spoken to their parents and they swear they did nothing of the sort."

There was a terrible plague, Sir, took all the children.

"...and some of the older lads were really very rude."

...some say they can still hear their little voices.

"One of them actually told me to bugger off!"

"Bugger off" they say, "Bugger offfff."

No. Even if he fell for it, it would only take one encounter with an enraged parent to undo all my good work. And then I really would be sunk.

I sought refuge in inanity.

"Now Sir," I looked kindly upon him; "you know what they say: boys will be horribly under-disciplined compared to girls who are expected to take up the slack socially even while bearing the brunt of their misbehaviour."

He blinked at me: "Is that what they say?"

"It's what I say. Still, I'm sure the lads will come round soon enough, once you get yourself settled in."

"Some of the girls were just as bad, you know."

"And I'm glad you noticed it, Sir." My hand, I realised, was still patting, presumably under some kind of shock-related compulsion. I schooled myself to stillness and gave him a final comforting smile: "I'm sure everyone will be much more reasonable once they've got to know you properly."

"Do you think?"

"A charming gentleman like you?" I crossed my fingers under my apron; "Of course they will. Now you just take a nice walk in this glorious sunshine, and everything will soon look much better."

My words were calm, but as I watched him go I was seething.

All my hard work. Wasted! The ingratitude of it all!

I snatched up the plates and bowls, dodged inside past Molly's avid gaze, dodged out again, turned a deaf ear to cries of "But Dora!" "It's your turn to man the bar!" and headed straight for the Rectory.

5

I went through the place like a fury: upturning furniture, hiding the candles *again* -there's nothing like a ghost with a fixed idea- splashing water all over the soft furnishings, and finally taking a breadknife to the ropes of his bed.

The knife already had a few chips in the blade before I started, probably as a casualty of our dense, Island bread, but by the time I had finished sawing and settled the mattress carefully back into place, the thing bore more than a passing resemblance to some of the older regulars back at the Inn, with barely a tooth to be seen and those that remained hanging on more out of stubbornness than anything else. Well I could hardly put it back on the bread board looking like that. If he got wind of somebody messing around with breadknives there would be no convincing the Reverend that the malevolent forces that - with any luck - spoiled his rest tonight were anything other than solidly human.

Mind you, if he carried on blaming the local children, their parents might just finish the job for me.

Parents in these parts are much like seagulls, and by that I don't just mean that they're loud, obnoxious and smell of fish.

The average proud papa or mama around here is far too busy to pay attention to small matters such as the nurture, education, or general welfare of their precious offspring. As such, infants, once weaned, are generally booted out of doors to amuse themselves until they are old enough to be of use getting in the harvest, or pulling a net. "No harm in a bit of fresh air and sunshine" they are told, or "You have to eat a peck of dirt before you die".

Any suggestion that perhaps, in that case, one could further prolong one's child's life by *not letting them eat dirt* is inevitably met by the blank glare of one who isn't at all sure what you just said, but who suspects that it was not a compliment.

So in general the children of the Island spend their days in a state of benign neglect, only interrupted when some fool comes across them in the act of stealing gooseberries, frightening cows, or pushing another child off a five hundred foot cliff, and makes the mistake of telling their parents.

At which point the unfortunate youth will find theirself on the receiving end of a screaming, bawling, fuming rage furious enough to rattle the shutters and loud enough to be heard from one end of the Island to the other.

This wrath, however, is as nothing compared to the pure, unadulterated fury that will descend upon the hapless idiot who opened their big mouth in the first place.

And then, inevitably, it will be decided that it wasn't really their child's fault in the first place, and blame will be placed on the child who first saw the gooseberry bush, or whose parents own the cow, or who is now lying in a broken heap at the bottom of the cliff. And life will go on as normal.

So it seemed to me that if he continued to blame our local darlings for the disturbances in his home, then no amount of pretended respect for the cloth would prevent their parents from unleashing the full force of their murderous ire in the Reverend Norman Poltwhistle's innocent, unsuspecting face. Before such a storm, braver heroes than he had fled, incontinently, never to be seen again.

Or rather they hadn't, because no-one had ever been so bloody stupid before, but they would have done, and so, with a bit of luck, would he.

With even more luck, it would be someone else's job to clean up the incontinence.

Of course, it was quite possible that someone would simply fillet him on the spot, sacrifice or no sacrifice.

No, I couldn't risk it: I was trying to save his life, not see him torn apart by a swarm of ravenous enraged parents. I took the knife out to the garden and threw it down the well instead.

Then, as an afterthought, I pulled up a bucket of water, dunked my boots in it until they were good and sodden, put them back on, and squelched a nice trail of muddy, waterlogged footprints back through the garden to the Rectory. Once there I took the boots off again and used them to continue the trail up the wall, over the mantelpiece and - standing on the table with one foot on the dresser for balance - straight across the ceiling and out again through the sealed and shuttered window.

Hah!

Let's see him blame that on the neighbour's children!

Finished at last, I wiped my muddy boots on his clean bedlinen, put them back on my feet, and scampered soggily back to the Inn to appease Molly.

I managed, barely, not to be late.

When I got back to the Inn Molly had, on slightly begrudgingly, put away my mop and bucket, set out the tables and benches, and made ready for an unexpected afternoon's work.

As I hove into view she gave a glad cry, embraced me in a brief but nonetheless disconcerting hug, and ran merrily off to do whatever she had planned to do with her day before her feckless friend went and wandered off without so much as a by-your-leave.

I had no idea what that actually was, mind you. Probably sitting on an outcrop, gazing at the fishing boats and mooning over whoever had replaced Jimmy the bastard Bettan in her perpetually optimistic affections. No doubt I'd hear all about it after it all fell apart.

Meanwhile, as Molly gallivanted off to adorn some rocky hillock, I secreted my slimy footwear behind the door, settled behind the bar, and did my best to pretend that my brain wasn't fizzing with mingled anxiety and anticipation.

The noontide crowd is never particularly large.

Our Island is a place of fishermen and farmers, none of them very successful. At this time of day most people would still be out pulling nets, or else snatching a meal in between performing the thousand and one jobs that are the difference between a barely successful farm and an abandoned wasteland.

In the afternoon, then, our patrons fell into roughly two groups: those who were so successful they could afford to take it easy while others tilled their fields and tended their stock, and those who were doing so very badly that a couple of hours snatched out of the best part of the day could hardly make things any worse. These were also, incidentally, two of the groups who took the most care in their devotions to the God.

It made sense, I supposed: those at the top were those with the most to lose, while those scraping along the bottom hadn't much hope of anything but maybe, just maybe, if the God smiled...

The two groups sat companionably about the taproom, conversing in winks and whispers, as happily sociable as if the shocking poverty of the latter was not directly linked to the conspicuous prosperity of the former. The landlords clearly enjoyed the opportunity to show their openhanded camaraderie, standing their rounds with the ease of those who had never had to count their pennies and talking with a winking, backslapping cheer of the better times that were just around the corner, just as long as everyone did their part, while the recipients of this goodwill notched up round after round on the slate in return, grinning all the while and assuring me that they'd soon be able to clear the lot. If they had dared speak a little louder, or more overtly, I was very much afraid that I should lose my temper.

Thankfully for my continued equilibrium, there was a third group in today, if a single person could be counted as a group, and that was Netta Stanley.

Netta had arrived on the Island some four years back and had instantly been identified as a candidate for the bonfire. She was slim and delicate as a willow, with light gingerish hair, fine clothes, and skin that had clearly never known a moment's labour or a day's rough weather in all her young life. She was also very clearly hiding from someone, and as such was perfectly placed to simply disappear from view. "A young lady your honour? And finely dressed? No, we've never had anyone of that sort here. We are but humble farmers." You get the idea.

Sadly everyone's hopes of a successful sacrifice at last were cruelly dashed when it was revealed that Netta, far from being a spotless virgin, was actually running away from a cruel marriage. After hearing this we had all expected her to stay for a few days, then run off again to seek shelter with some well-placed relative or other, or at least to hide herself in some more comfortable location, but to everyone's surprise she stayed, and *stayed*.

She cut off the shimmering curtain of her hair and tied back what remained with a length of twine. She sold the fine silken gowns and bought homespun shifts and serviceable petticoats. She shocked everyone on the Island by applying for work as a labourer up at Miser Farm - so called because the ground there is rich as anything but no matter how much work you put in you'll barely get anything out - and shocked us again by not only getting the job but keeping it.

These days Netta was tall, wiry and tanned, with strong hands and a quiet, confident smile. She looked so unlike the fragile, lost girl who had come ashore four years before that I suspected if an angry husband ever did come seeking her here, he would look right through her and never recognise her at all.

I had no idea why she was in the Inn that afternoon, but I was grateful to her all the same, for as long as she was there, a technical outsider in our midst, nobody would dare say anything about the ruddy sacrifice.

So they kept to their hints and gestures, and smiled at one another, and drank their beer, united in their interest in trussing up poor Norman Poltwhistle for a little reverend rotisserie.

Said Reverend made no appearance that afternoon.

I was glad not to see him: whether he was still out walking in the halfhearted sunshine, or whether he had returned to discover the haunted wreck of his home, I didn't know, but I knew that if once I saw him I would be incapable of keeping the suspense and anticipation from showing in my face.

It was bad enough as it was, squelching about in my stockings as I distributed cups and pint pots, hearing the avid murmurs on every side, surrounded by the happy, open smiles of those anticipating the gruesome spectacle to come.

Now I'm not the cleverest person in the world, I know, and I doubt I'm the best educated even on the Island -even taking into account my mother's books, and the Poet doing his best while he was there- but I have always been, as my Gammer used to say, just that bit too clever for my own damn good. Naturally suspicious is how I prefer to put it. Just downright bloody-minded is the Island diagnosis.

Whatever it is, it made me look twice at some of those cheerful, smiling faces; especially those of the wealthier landowners; or the men with two or even three boats to their names, who hadn't so much as set a hand to an oar in over a year.

It wasn't all of them, not even most, but here and there among that cheerful throng I spotted it: that bluff, hearty, all-in-this-together bonhomie, with that extra little twinkle in the eye that said: "And as long as they're all thinking about setting fire to him, no-one's asking how it is that *I've* got so much while *they've* got so little".

No-one would have believed me if I'd said anything, mind. It would have been The Rights Of Man all over again.

I remembered Gammer talking, years ago, about the last sacrifice, back in her own Gammer's day.

"It was terrible bad my Poppet," she sighed; "Ground tough as nails and nothing to put in it anyway. And the sea giving up nothing but weeds and salt." She'd twitched a little at the thought, and cuddled me close in her bony arms, as if to somehow shield me from starvation.

"But they knew what must be done." She continued, and my wide infant eyes had caught on hers, still so warm and comforting even clouded white with age.

"They knew," she rocked me closer yet; "they knew, and when a lull came in the storm the men took a boat to the mainland and hauled back some young thing as was out too late, and made a properly reverent offering of her. She kicked like anything, they say, when the flames picked up, but the God took her soon enough."

"And did that make everything better again?" I'd piped, only half understanding what I'd heard.

"Not at once, my sweeting," she beamed; "but they burned another the next year, and another one year after that, and soon after that the waves calmed and the harvests began to come good again. So you see," and she'd dandled me on her lap; "the bonfire brought everything right again."

There's no arguing with logic like that.

By the end of the afternoon I was tired, anxious, and just this side of irritable. It had come on to rain again at some point, and when Molly finally came in, it was with about half the Island's mud sloughing from her skirts.

"God of the harvest, it isn't half blowing out there!" She dripped across to the fireplace and stood, steaming lightly, wringing out her hair.

"Is it?" I asked, weakly, gazing in dismay at the thick muddy trail that had draggled all across the hitherto gleaming flagstones.

"Like a typhoon," Molly twirled around, more mud spattering in every direction, to warm her dainty backside over the fire; "No-one'll be taking a boat out tonight, that's for certain. We'll have them all in here instead, knocking back the ale and maundering on about the sacrifice."

"Oh!" She clapped a hand to her pretty mouth; "Sorry Dor' I wasn't thinking."

She sludged her way across the room again and enveloped me in a moist embrace.

"Don't you worry about your Reverend: you'll have him disqualified in no time."

She patted my back in a comforting sort of way, having apparently taken my horrified expression for one of fear for my supposed paramour.

Eventually, and with some difficulty, I disentangled myself from her kindly arms and after a few abortive attempts at rational speech, gestured helplessly at the floor.

It took a few moments for Molly to make the connection between the freshly scrubbed floor of this morning and the burgeoning swamp now before us, but as reality set in she erupted in a babble of self-recrimination. I let the flow of words wash over me, not really listening, until I caught a half-formed offer to scrub it all again.

"Would you really Moll'?" I broke into her stream of consciousness with ruthless gratitude; "It'd be such help. And you know," I perked up as a thought struck me; "if you deal with the floor I can wash those muddy things for you."

It was Molly's turn to be rendered speechless.

I could see her point: theoretically we shared the Inn's various labours between us but, neither of us having the strength to easily handle the sodden clothes, or to weld the awkward weight of the washing dolly, and nobody caring to endure the clinging, ammonia-scented steam and heat of the copper itself, avoiding the laundry had by now become something of a matter of honour. Our usual practice was to pass the job frantically off between us until nobody had a shift to stand up in, at which point the awful duty would fall upon whomever could not contrive to be inescapably busy on that day.

Which was to say that generally Molly did it.

If I were forced to choose between feeding a pill to the bloody cockerel and doing the laundry...

Well, I'd choose the laundry, but I wouldn't be happy about it.

On more than one occasion we had conspired to convince a somewhat woozy Tom that the copper and stick were an experimental mash tub: a ruse that worked very well, right up until he tried to bottle the supposed beer. There are still a few bottles of Laundress' Old Peculiar knocking about the Inn.

Get a body drunk enough and they'll drink anything.

So I could understand Molly's sudden confusion.

Right now, though, I needed to do the wash by myself: I had a bed full of mysteriously muddy sheets upstairs, not to mention the various charcoal smudges left behind by the ghost of Anna Matilda, and my still soggy stockings. The whole pile would be inescapably incriminating were anyone to blunder upon it by chance, but a few armloads of Molly's mud-stained finery thrown in with the rest of it should disguise my guilty linens nicely.

By the time I'd managed to convince Molly that yes, I really did mean it, and no this wasn't some kind of cunning plan to leave her with every subsequent batch of laundry for the rest of my life, and no, I hadn't hit my head on anything, or got a touch of the non-existent sun, or drunk Tom's latest "experimental" ale, there was barely time to bundle the lot of it into a tub to soak, throw on a pair of clean stockings and get back downstairs to open up again for the night.

I'd half hoped, as I tripped down the stairs with blessedly clean, dry feet, that I would find the floor swabbed to shining once again, but by the time the first of the night's customers pushed through the door Molly was still upstairs, unpinning her hair and arranging a fresh skirt and bodice to achieve just the right amount of tempting bedraggle, and the floor was still a miserable, mud-spattered mess.

I consoled myself with the thought that, even if they did notice it, no-one would care but me.

The evening passed much like the afternoon, only more so, with the religious enthusiasms somewhat muffled under the general burble about nets and crops and daily life, liberally sprinkled with old anecdotes, and even older jokes. As a rule the repetitive drone of it all bored me half to tears, but tonight, given the alternative, it was almost as great a relief as the soft, dry stockings and unmuddied slippers warming my chilly feet. Even so, as I passed through the crowd with my trays and tankards I heard far too many remarks about bad harvests and good, and the one sure way to turn the tide in our favour.

For every harmless ramble about the weather, every wildly embroidered reminiscence, every argument over the best way to make bloody *soup*, there was a conspiratorial mutter about rope, or trusses of wood, or the inexpressible benevolence of the Island God.

I should have known better than to wish that they would stop. But I didn't, and so I did, and then they did. All at once. Because the blessed Reverend Poltwhistle had walked into the bar.

Once he had finished blinking idiotically on the threshold, and I had finished gazing in awe at the magnificent subtlety of my compatriots, he made his way to his usual table opposite the door, and I hurried over to see what I could persuade him to drink. In doing so I noticed a large portmanteau by his side: just the sort of thing a gentleman might want if he needed to pack up all his worldly goods and flee into the night.

I swallowed my suddenly bubbling glee and in a *perfectly normal voice* enquired as to whether he would be wanting any ale this evening, Sir?

"Are you alright?" He asked, concernedly.

"Me Sir? Fine Sir! Very well indeed, Sir! Can I get you anything to drink, Sir?" *Or a boat off the Island, perhaps.*

"Only I have some lozenges somewhere, if you would care for one: your voice sounds terribly strained."

I coughed, as unobtrusively as possible. Somehow this only made matters worse.

In as calm, squeakless and unstrained a tone as I could summon, I once more asked whether, this being, in fact, an inn, he might like to order a beverage of some kind, if only to add to the general ambience.

"You can just hold it, Sir, if you find you don't care for it."

Acknowledging that my reasoning in this matter was sound, he consented to be brought half a pint of mild ale.

"But are you quite sure that you are well, Dora? I must say, now that I see you properly you do look awfully tired."

My instinct was to stand by my claim to blooming good health, but on second thought I remembered the dark, sleepless circles under my eyes, and allowed that I might have just the tiniest bit of a headache.

"A headache?"

"Yes, Sir, just a touch." I turned on him a gaze of open honesty: "I am but a simple Island girl" it said. "I have no reason to lie to you" it added. "Nor guile to carry it off" it persuaded, cunningly. "And for your information," it put in; "a headache could absolutely cause a sore throat. And a cough. What do you know, anyway? You're a preacher, not a surgeon."

I went to fetch him his drink before I could stare anything I might regret.

At the bar I took a deep, calming breath, then another, then stopped before I could start to hyperventilate. I grabbed a bottle more or less at random and slopped it into a fairly clean looking mug. Then I took one more, slow, deliberate breath and made my way with furious sobriety back to the Reverend's table.

"Dear me, Sir" I said, with studied nonchalance; "what a terribly big bag you have there. Not leaving us already, I hope?" And I paused, sympathetically.

Now he could tell me all about the awful disturbances in his home, and how he could stand it no more, and could I possibly point him in the direction of someone who would be willing to row him across to the-

"Oh no," he beamed; "quite the reverse."

"The reverse?" An icy chill ran down my back.

Since the chill was immediately followed by the familiar slamming of the door, it was probably just a draft from outside. The awful sense of foreboding, however, stayed.

"Whatever do you mean by that?"

"Ah," he looked at me conspiratorially, over his glasses; "You recollect that I was having a little trouble with some of the local children?"

I remembered my accidental frame-up, yes.

I nodded uncomfortably.

"Well, I'm afraid things came to rather a head after I left you this morning: some harsh words with a few of their parents, nothing terrible, but I was rather wondering if I should seek some other lodging. Absence makes the heart grow fonder, as they say, and good walls make good neighbours, so perhaps if I wasn't quite so much on their doorstep..."

There are very few good walls on the Island, as the ground is so waterlogged that even the soundest foundations tend to sag after a few years. Still, I agreed that I might be much fonder of a good many people if only they would be somewhere that I wasn't, and I nodded as though I understood him perfectly.

"So I spoke with the landlord, ah, Tom, isn't it? And he said I could move in tonight!"

"Move...in Sir?"

"Yes!"

"Move in where?"

"Why, here of course."

I was momentarily dumbstruck. I stood, gaping like a fish left too long on the dock, the Reverend's mug still held aimlessly aloft.

Fortunately he completely misread this sudden turn for statuehood.

"Now, I know you don't very often have guests, and I'm not expecting very much. A warm, dry room with congenial company will suit me very well indeed. And I already know the company's congenial. I dare swear I shall have nothing to complain about." And he patted my nerveless hand.

"You say that now," I heard myself say; "But Molly snores fit to bring the roof down."

"Does she really?" He twinkled at me.

"Well, so I hear." Oh cannibal god what was I saying? "But then she's hardly ever in her own bed, so I don't have much chance to judge."

"Well in that case, I'm sure I won't have any problem at all." He gave me a most un-vicar-like grin.

"I'm...sure you won't, Sir."

I finally forced myself to lower his mug to the table, my hand trembling so that I slopped a good third of it over the brim, and stumbled blankly back to the security of the bar.

Once there I left Molly to handle the customers, and pretended to busy myself among the bottles while I frantically sorted through my disordered thoughts.

He wasn't leaving.

I hadn't scared him away.

He did not, in fact, seem to realise that he should have been scared.

He showed no inclination whatsoever towards changing his mind on this matter.

I was rapidly running out both of ideas and of clean stockings.

I was fairly sure that I couldn't manage another night spent haunting his house without falling asleep in the middle of the day.

Probably in the middle of some awkward task or other.

Like emptying the slop bucket.

Or raking out the coals.

Or...

I pulled myself back from a morbid fantasy wherein I keeled over in the middle of doing the laundry and pitched headfirst into the scalding copper - a horrible death, it's true, but at least I wouldn't be the one to clean up the mess- with the reminder that it didn't matter whether I was up to haunting his house or not.

Because he wasn't in his house.

He was here.

He was here, in the Inn, with his stupid bag and his stupid smile, and his stupid bloody happiness at having some decent company for once.

By which he meant me.

Oh no.

Oh, *no.*

There was no way I was going to be able to haunt him out of the Inn.

I couldn't do it.

I couldn't and quite honestly even if I could I didn't think I *could*.

Oh no.

Oh, bugger.

Oh great, bloody, hell spawned and hideous, blue eyed balls of the ever-hungry God.

Oh *help*.

I was going to have to seduce him.

6

Right.

I could do this.

I mean, how hard could it be?

The answer, it seemed, was very hard indeed.

The thing was, I'd never put much thought into that side of things before. And by "much" I meant "any". It had just never interested me.

I mean, I knew the theory: even if half the Island hadn't spent every summer merrily tripping behind haystacks and hedges, to emerge rumpled, beaming and somewhat muddy, you couldn't spend much time in the proximity of Molly without gaining a fairly firm grounding in every permutation of what went where. But I'd just never been able to care about any of it.

I'd said as much to the Poet, who'd agreed that if I found myself immune to his blandishments there was probably no hope for me, and then suggested, with surprising delicacy, that perhaps I was turning my attentions in the wrong direction.

I replied that while I appreciated his concern I would turn *his* attention once more to my remarks concerning Molly and my proximity thereto, as I suspected that if I hadn't suffered any sort of awakening yet in regards to *her* munificent charms then there probably wasn't anything to awake. He'd conceded cheerfully, and returned to inventing rude last lines for Shakespeare's more uninspiring sonnets.

So while I understood what people *did*, I didn't really have any idea how they got there, let alone why they wanted to.

Molly never seemed to want for admirers, but I couldn't see that she did anything in particular to attract them: she just did her job and maybe smiled a little, and men flocked to her like fluff to a particularly sticky honeypot.

I could always ask her, I supposed, but then I'd have to explain that the Reverend and I weren't really deep in some blissful summery romance after all. I just didn't think I could break her heart like that. And asking anyone else would, quite aside from the crushing embarrassment *and* the whole plotting-to-betray-our-beloved-Island-God thing, mean admitting to what I didn't do with Davey Mullins. Which might well end with two for the barbecue instead of one.

No: ask no questions, tell no pyromaniac zealots.

Molly must do something, I reasoned: it wasn't as though she just went off with whichever fellow presented himself. Well, not all the time.

I'd seen her mooning over one idiot or another more times than I could count: gazing out of windows, humming little songs to herself, talking complete rubbish to the chickens when she came to lug out their feed. It was always the same, time and again: she'd waft around like a wet blanket for about a week and then she'd manage to catch their eye over the bar or something, and then it would all be rainbows and buttercups until, inevitably, another name joined the roster of heartbreaking, heartless bastards.

Was there a special *look* or something? It never looked like much to me: maybe she lowered her eyelids a little, or stared a bit harder, but that was it.

Come to think of it, the Poet never wanted for company either, and he just used to sit there, glowering smugly to himself until some daft girl decided to fling herself at him.

"His brooding look" Molly called it, and to be fair he did somewhat resemble a hen sitting on a particularly beloved egg.

Could I do that? I risked a glance across the room. Reverend Poltwhistle was regarding his mug of beer as if it was an especially large spider that he didn't want to share the table with but couldn't quite bring himself to squash.

I lowered my eyelids.

He fiddled with his mug.

I stared harder.

He resumed moping.

I imitated the aspect of a chicken.

He looked up.

I focused every ounce of willpower into my eyes and glared at him along the bridge of my nose.

He looked straight at me.

I rebounded in panic and crashed into a shelf-full of mugs.

There was a round of ironic applause, during which the Reverend Norman "Awkward" Poltwhistle shifted uncomfortably before returning to the morbid contemplation of his ale.

Right, I told myself firmly, you got his attention once. Now pull yourself together and try again! I shoved the disarranged crockery into some hasty semblance of order and affected a casual saunter back to the bar. Once there I leaned one elbow on the bartop, rested my head upon my hand at as fetching an angle as I could manage, and tried again.

There was a coughing sound somewhere above my head. I ignored it and intensified my gaze.

He was looking in my direction! This was it! I narrowed my vision to a point and attempted a smoulder.

The coughing redoubled.

I considered offering one of the Reverend's lozenges.

"Look, are you going to sell me a ruddy drink or what?"

I groaned and stood up. I was getting a crick in my neck from all that leaning anyway.

By the time I'd served everyone, and then served everyone who turned up while I was serving the first lot, and *then* made the mistake of catching Old Man Morris' eye, walked through the bar to serve him, taken half a dozen orders from all the people I passed getting there and back, argued with Rely Shepherd over their bar tab, and then dealt with everyone who'd piled up at the bar in my absence, he'd stopped looking at me.

You know, some people have no sticking power.

Still, I managed to seize his attention a fair few times throughout the night, despite the customers' best attempts to distract me, and I made a few useful observations along the way.

To begin with, I couldn't just stand there staring: people would notice, and even if they were too self-centred to find anything odd about it, they would get in the way, or cough at me, or wave a hand in front of my face and expect me to fetch them things.

A better approach was to go at it sidelong: glance his way while I was delivering a tray of drinks and just happen to catch his eye, or meet his gaze over a couple of pint pots only to look bashfully away the moment I "noticed".

Secondly, it was important not to open the eyes too far: a too-wide gaze felt as though I had engaged in some sort of staring competition, and had the unfortunate effect of drying out the eyeballs.

While recovering from this, I also discovered that while delicately fluttering lashes may sound good in books, in reality they just make it impossible to see anything and, if fluttered too frantically or too long, can result in a blinding headache.

No, half-closed eyes, a casual yet consistent smoulder, and above all the element of surprise. That was the way to go about it.

I liked the word "smoulder". I'd never really understood it in this context before, and when I encountered it in books, had taken to mentally replacing it with "Molly" or "Poet" as appropriate. "She Mollyed at him enticingly"

"The prince turned a Poeting glare upon his captor"

"The coals Poeted in the hearth". That sort of thing.

But now I tried it for myself I felt I understood: a smoulder was a warm sort of look, that felt as though if it were given any encouragement at all something must burst into flames.

I ignored the possibility that said thing would be my face, and smouldered determinedly all over the Inn.

By the time we came to last orders I had managed at least a dozen good smoulders and got in a couple of burning looks that I was particularly proud of. I had also accidentally snubbed about a quarter of our regular clientele and was holding back a blush you could fry an egg on. But never mind that: the important thing was that the disobligingly staunch Reverend Norman "Awkward" Poltwhistle was well and truly *captivated*.

I felt his eyes upon me as I whisked about the common room, and wondered at the sense of power it gave me.

Was this, I asked myself as I poured an obstinately loyal customer out of the door and closed it firmly in his face, how Molly felt all the time? Powerful, beautiful, filled with elation and a vague sense of annoyance at being expected to actually do her job?

Well, no, she was far too good-hearted for that. And a lot better at dodging than I was.

All the same, it was with a sense of beguiling self-satisfaction that I sauntered idly up to the Reverend's table and prepared to accept his advances.

He rose to the occasion beautifully - and literally - jumping to his feet as I approached and splashing what little beer he hadn't already spilled all over his shirt.

"Now, Reverend" I murmured in the smokiest tones I could muster; "You've spoiled your good linen."

"Oh, ah have I?" he stammered nervily.

"Indeed you have" I leaned a little closer; "I should take that off if I was you sir, before it's stained for good."

"Why that's, um, very thoughtful of you Miss - ah - Miss Dora"

"Call me Dora, Sir" I smiled enticingly.

"Dora then. Do you think, Dora, that if I were to give you this shirt you might be able to wash it for me?"

I was somewhat nonplussed.

"Only I did notice rather a lot of washing piled up in that little room next to the copper.

I'm sure it couldn't be much trouble to just slip in there and add another shirt to the pile"

Ah, I recognised this gambit: I'd agree, we'd sneak away so he could "give me his shirt" and then I'd *do his laundry*.

Or he'd do mine, I supposed.

"Why Sir" I rejoined as saucily as I could muster, "I'm sure *that* will be no trouble at all"

Was that the right thing to say? I wasn't at all sure: perhaps I should have implied that he'd have been a *lot* of trouble, terrible amounts of trouble, *huge, throbbing trouble Sir*.

The thing was that now that push came to shove I found I was even less keen on either push *or* shove than I had previously realised. In fact the whole idea was starting to make me rather queasy.

Maybe I could get him to turn his back while he undressed, and then belt him over the head with the washing dolly? Then when he came round I could pretend he'd finished already and then passed out.

Regretfully, I abandoned the idea: he hadn't drunk nearly enough to believe a story like that, and besides, with my luck I wouldn't just knock him senseless, I'd knock him dead. Which would put something of a crimp in the whole saving-his-life plan.

I swallowed a mouthful of bile and steeled myself to the inevitable: "Well then, if you wanted to *give me your shirt*, it's just this way sir." And I turned to lead him to the laundry room.

"Oh, I - ah - thought I could just leave it outside my room"

"Your room, Sir?" Well, a bed would be preferable to dirty laundry I supposed.

"Yes, once I've settled in: the stain won't set straight away if I soak it in my wash basin, and it would save me walking through the inn without a shirt on."

The conversation seemed to be running strangely away from me. I seized the reins and attempted to haul it back on track.

"Of course, Sir, won't you come this way then and I'll show you to your room."

I slunk as seductively as I could over to the door to the stairway, and waited for him to heave his baggage up onto his shoulder.

As I led him up the stairs I did my best to keep his mind on the matter at hand, despite the difficulties of getting a tall and ungainly gentleman with a large and bulky bag, up a steep, narrow staircase that had been designed more as a trap for the unwary than as a means of travelling between floors.

In the end, though, after my third attempt at innuendo had been wasted while he chased after his dropped luggage, I gave up imitating a seductress, squeezed my way back past him, thrust the bag into his arms and, spinning him back to face the stairs set my hands firmly against his posterior and pushed.

He shot up the staircase like, well, less like a cork from a bottle and more like a tall and gangling man of the cloth falling unexpectedly *up* a confined and corkscrewing flight of stairs while clutching a heavily bulging holdall in both arms.

He toppled over at the top, but at least the bag broke his fall.

"Now, Sir" I drawled, trying frantically to get the situation back under control; "That wasn't how I'd planned on getting my hands on you *at all*."

He stood up and blinked at me dazedly: "What was that?"

"Um." Oh lumme, I didn't think I could say it again.

"Your room's just over here, Sir," I waved weakly toward the door then rallied somewhat; "Next to mine." I heaved the bag up and presented it to him: "I think you'll be particularly pleased with the *bed*, Sir."

"Oh, really? I'd assumed, that is, I mean, I'm terribly glad to hear that." And he took the bag into his arms, walked through the door and closed it behind him.

I stood, stymied, where I had stopped.

What was I supposed to do? Had I misread the situation? Didn't he want me?

I felt strangely insulted at the idea.

I mean, I might not have *wanted* to be wanted but I still wanted to be *wanted*. Or at least I wanted him to want me to want him. If you see what I mean.

Or maybe I hadn't been mistaken. Maybe I'd just missed something, some hint he'd thrown out that would tell me what to do, some subtle suggestion that was supposed to convey everything.

Or what if he hadn't said anything because I was just supposed to know?

Maybe this was something people just understood. Maybe in this situation anyone but me would just *know* that I was supposed to follow him inside, or go and wait for him in my own bed, or...go and hide in the bloody laundry room?!

Maybe that sort of knowledge just came with the territory: *"Interested in an intimate acquaintance with another person's wobbly bits? Here, have an uncontrollable tendency to blush at random, an innate understanding of smouldering, and the ability to know what you're supposed to do when your would-be swain shuts the door in your face."*

Fortunately, while I was panicking he opened the door again.

"Yes, that all looks very satisfactory, thank you so much"

"You're...welcome, Sir?"

As I scrabbled for something vaguely provocative to say, he beamed at me "Well, goodnight!" And he closed the door again.

Wait a minute! Before I could think what I was doing I hammered on the door.

He opened it at once. "Was there something else?"

Well I had thought you might want to throw me down on either your very satisfactory bed or a pile of dirty laundry and have your somewhat distasteful way with me, Sir.

"Ah." I said, helpfully.

He looked at me interrogatively.

No, this would never do. I was starting to sound like him.

"It's just, I noticed you looking at me a couple of times... downstairs...Sir...and I wondered if there was something you wanted?"

And why, I wondered somewhat wildly, had I felt the need to turn that into a question? Be more assertive Dora, for goodness sakes!

"Ah." Oh, good, now *he* was feeling uncomfortable again, too.

"Sir?"

"Well, as it happens *I'd* noticed you looking at *me*".

Oh, good, maybe I could salvage this situation after all.

"Or rather" he smiled confidingly "I'd noticed you *not* looking at me."

No, the prospects for a salvage operation were looking bleak. I had no idea what was going on here at all.

"Not...looking, sir?"

"Because you couldn't *see* me, could you Dora?".

And with that the situation foundered and went down with all hands.

I answered at random "No?"

He grinned at me.

He had quite a nice smile, I noticed, when he wasn't awash with nerves.

Or maybe he just enjoyed driving innocent young seductresses to babbling confusion.

"I could see you squinting at me from the other side of the bar".

Squinting!

"Oh don't look so dismayed."

Dismayed? I was *insulted*.

"Here, try these" and he plucked the glasses from his nose and settled them on mine!

The world dissolved into a blur of shapes and colours.

"There you go!" he beamed foggily at me "That's better isn't it"

"What in the world?" I was talking to myself but fortunately he thought he understood.

"Ah, of course, I should have explained: these are called *eyeglasses*, they're quite common where I live so I hadn't realised you wouldn't recognise them".

Wonderful: instead of a sinister seductress I was now a myopic yokel.

"Well sir" I heard myself utter, faintly "They do say as how the mainland is full of spectacles."

"Do they indeed?"

Oh cadaverous lord was that a chuckle?

"Well, I can't let you keep this pair I'm afraid, but perhaps I shall be able to find you something suitable once I'm back home."

And with that he tweaked the specs back off of my nose again and set his hand to the door: "Now I really must get some sleep, it's fearfully late and it's been a terribly long day. Goodnight Dora."

He yawned into his room then stopped in the act of closing the door: "Oh, and Dora?"

"Yes, Sir?"

"I'll leave the shirt outside your door, shall I?"

7

That seemed to be that for that little seduction scene.

I slumped wearily into the room I shared with Molly, and collapsed into bed.

If this had been one of my novels I would have been the very picture of a tragic, lovelorn maiden. As it was I was mostly just miserably frustrated.

Mind you, if this had been one of my novels then he would have been the one doing the seducing, not me.

Barmaids in books, when we were mentioned at all, were usually buxom wenches whose role was to provide background repartee and to remind the reader how terribly attractive the hero supposedly was. Should such a wench be particularly fortunate, she might be permitted to bring some simple nourishment to a pair of fleeing lovers, or perhaps have her petticoats stolen by a daring gentleman in need of a disguise.

On those rare occasions when one did feature in a seduction somewhere, it was inevitably as an unfortunate prior victim of the villainous gentleman with the sardonic eye and twirling moustaches, cast off when he set his sights on the innocent - and wealthy - heroine. Whether the barmaid had been likewise innocent was never much discussed.

Ladies might sometimes be seductresses, of course, providing they were elegant ladies with velvet gowns and glossy black tresses falling from widows peaks, but barmaids had neither the wealth nor the wardrobe for the job.

No, literary convention made it clear that my role was that of the tragic seducee. It was just typical that in reality I was expected to handle everything myself.

Mind you, I couldn't exactly see the Right Reverend Norman Poltwhistle in the role of an infamous seducer.

I briefly imagined him with a set of twisty moustaches and a sneer, and was abruptly distracted from my sulk by a fit of the giggles. I tried adding the sardonic gaze, but was hampered rather by the fact that I wasn't honestly sure what "sardonic" meant. I wondered if it was anything like "flinty".

Musing on this, and on the numerous iniquities of fiction I drowsed away.

I awoke next morning with the kind of heavy, bone-deep weariness that so often follows a single good night's sleep after any period of sleeplessness.

Stay here my blankets insisted, we'*ll keep you safe and warm.*

That's all well and good, I thought, but I'm working to a deadline here and if I don't get up and do something soon, that poor innocent clergyman will end up very dead indeed.

Or, suggested the mattress, *maybe if you just go back to sleep it will all have sorted itself out and you won't have anything to worry about at all.*

"Well that doesn't sound very likely, now does it?" I muttered into my pillow.

Why not? asked the pillow, beguilingly, *anything's possible. Look: Molly's already got up and fed the chickens.*

At this I bolted upright in alarm and looked about the room. It was true: Molly was nowhere to be seen.

Now this absence alone would have been no cause for concern, for Molly was rarely in her own bed by the time the sun came up, but as I glanced around the room I saw that she clearly had been there. Her clean skirt and bodice were gone from the chest in the corner, the blankets that last night were all higgledy piggledy confusion had been drawn up and smoothed carefully, if inexpertly, out. Most suspicious yet, the heap of dirty linen that had been steadily growing in the corner of our room was nowhere to be seen.

I shook off my bedcovers and ran to look out of the window. To my horror the tiny pane of glass was clear and bright and my nose was assailed with the pungent scent of vinegar.

She'd cleaned it!

In the yard the chickens were head down in their mash and Molly was tripping daintily across the gleamingly clean flagstones to the brewing shed with a covered tray balanced on one hand.

She made an appallingly charming picture.

That bloody cockerel didn't even try to peck at her.

With a sense of deep foreboding I dragged myself away from the glass and dressed for the day then opened the door and, in the ever growing certainty of my impending doom, gathered the Reverend's soggy shirt from the floor and crept apprehensively down the stairs.

In the taproom the floor gleamed damply, a pot of porridge sang merrily above a crackling fire, and every window shone. Last night's tankards, I noticed, were still scattered about the room, but the general impression was nonetheless one of enthusiastic Spring-cleaning.

The door swung merrily open and Molly came skipping into the inn, beaming all over her perfect face.

"Good morning Dora!" she sang.

"Don't you "Good morning" me" I retorted: "I know what you're up to"

"Why whatever can you mean, Dor'?" She looked at me with wide, guileless eyes.

She didn't fool me. Only one thing would make Molly attack the day's labours with more than the absolute minimum of effort, let alone anything approaching eagerness. I looked down at the damp linen in my hand, then back to her inexorably smiling face.

The laundry.

"But Dora" you may be thinking; "Didn't you *offer* to do the laundry of your very own accord, not two chapters ago?"

And the answer is yes, yes I did, but that didn't mean I had to be happy about it.

Indeed, the very knowledge that I *had* offered to do the laundry, that in fact I *needed* to do the laundry, and to do it all by myself, only rankled all the worse. In the usual way of things I could bargain or barter, palm a few of my most hated tasks off on Molly in exchange for some of hers, and maybe conspire with her to make Tom help with the worst of it or, in extremis, to bury the truly irredeemable items behind the henhouse and deny all knowledge of their existence.

But no. Today I had to do the whole boiling lot of it myself. And be *grateful* for it.

It would have helped if Molly had been even the tiniest bit smug, but she wasn't. She was just her usual, sweet, good-natured self: a little baffled that I was apparently seized with some inescapable urge to take on the hardest, heaviest, most miserable work we had in exchange for her simply doing a small part of her job for once, but perfectly happy to uphold her end of the bargain and, apparently, more.

I glared at her and stalked off to the laundry room, the wet shirt squelching sulkily in my hand.

What we called the laundry room was really more of a shed bolted onto the side of the building.

The roof was high at one end, to accommodate the big copper tub and a couple of rather helplessly optimistic washing lines strung up across the ceiling, then sloped down almost to ground level at the other. In the low outer wall there were a couple of windows set, to let in air and let out steam.

If you have ever watched a kettle boil, you will have some idea of exactly how well this didn't work.

The great copper that dominated the room was already filling the air with a soft, drifting thread of vapour, and against the low wall the shallow rinsing trough was freshly filled with cool clear water.

The bleaching pail was also freshly filled.

I do not want to talk about the bleaching pail.

As I glanced about the room I could see that everything was ready and waiting for me so, seeing no way in which to forestall the inevitable, I rolled up my sleeves, hung my good bodice on a peg out of the way, and set to work.

I took the lid off the copper and dumped in a couple of good handfuls of coarse lye soap - the same soap used for everything on the Island, from scrubbing floors to washing unruly infants - then heaved in the first load of linens and picked up the washing dolly.

A washing dolly looks like a little, three-legged stool, from the middle of which sprouts a tall, sturdy pole. Standing against the wall it resembled nothing so much as a torture device from one of my mother's more unpleasant books. Even the name "washing dolly" sounded unpleasantly euphemistic to my ears. I seized the implement by its handle and proceeded to interrogate the laundry.

Pummelling a mass of cloth in a tub full of water is hard work, even when the room isn't flooded with steam: linen isn't so very light to begin with, but as it takes on water it becomes almost unbearably heavy. Add to this the perverse pleasure clothes seem to take in sinking to the bottom when you want to pull them up, then filling with air and floating when you need to push them down, and the general tendency of everything to wrap itself around the washing dolly and tie itself in knots, and you have a nightmare beyond anything in the Discoverie Of Witchcraft.

The long handle of the dolly gave me some additional leverage and purchase on the clothes, but even so as I leaned over the water to haul them up again, I felt I was as likely to pitch straight into the tub myself as I was to pull them out. Still I struggled on, belabouring load after load of bedlinens and breeches, shifts and smallclothes.

The water seethed and roiled under my hands, and the cramped room filled with thick, rolling fog, so that my shift clung to my skin and my hands slipped on the long wooden shaft as I worked the heavy loads again and again, up and down and up and down. My head throbbed in the heat and airlessness.

Finally, I heaved the last, great, impossibly heavy mass from the copper to the rinsing trough, and raked my straggling hair out of my eyes as I searched the cloudy water for errant handkerchiefs.

* * *

And then the door opened and Norman Poltwhistle wandered in.

My first, wild thought was that perhaps he had come to seduce me after all.

My second was that no novelist would ever put her romantic leads in such a position: I was half-dressed and soaked through with sweat and steam, my shift clinging to my skin, my hair curling wetly about my face and shoulders, and my cheeks blazing crimson in the heat. There was absolutely nothing appealing about my appearance.

Still, if he had decided to have his wicked, moustache twirling way with me on a pile of sodden sheets then I would just have to make the best of it and hope nothing got indelibly stained in the process.

And try to steer him away from the corner with the bleaching pail.

But no, he just smiled his usual anxious smile, and stood there in the doorway, wiping the steam off his glasses.

"Ah, Dora!" He remarked, once he was quite sure he could see me, "I was hoping I'd find you here".

If your next words are "Could I just pop this into the wash? I'm sure it won't be any trouble" I thought, smiling welcomingly, *I shall brain you with the washing dolly.*

"Were you, sir? Why, how very fortunate" I said instead, and he beamed as if he had done something immensely clever instead of just tracking me down to the exact location he had already known I would be in.

"Yes. I was wondering if you might like to take a walk with me"

"*Now*, sir?" I stood there, dripping with soapsuds and dirty water, staring at him.

Finally, a clear romantic overture and I was entirely unable to accept it. Even if I were to leave the great pile of soggy linen to moulder, I was not remotely ready for an afternoon of romantic strolling through the drizzly countryside. Yet now, in the middle of all the steam, and suds and chaos, *now* he invited me to take a walk with him?

I was caught wrong-footed and unprepared.

I was a thousand miles from even imitating a witty, flirtatious conversationalist.

I was wet, I was dirty and I was tired.

I was a miserable mass of indignities scarcely fit to be seen in private, let alone public.

I was bloody livid was what I was.

"No, not just now."

Oh. My temper cooled somewhat: an impressive feat in this kettle of a room.

"Only you mentioned that the island had a great many odd carvings and so on, and I wondered whether you would care to show me one or two?"

He looked rather unsure of himself: I wondered whether he had noticed my annoyance, or whether he was simply unused to asking women out.

It briefly occurred to me that perhaps he was worrying that the inherent power balance between our relative roles and stations in life could leave me unable to meaningfully give or refuse consent to his proposition. But that was ridiculous: no one thought like that.

I brushed the idea aside and plunged into the breach: "Of course, Sir, I should be delighted to go with you! What a very charming idea, indeed."

As I watched him turn faintly pink - whether from the heat or the encouragement I couldn't tell - I calculated frantically: three days left till the ceremony and I'd need at least one of those to seduce him properly, one more in case he really was as oblivious as he appeared, another to knock him over the head and drag him off somewhere if things went really, truly, inescapably wrong and..."Would tomorrow morning be too soon Sir?" He looked at me with an air of mild reproof: "Tomorrow is Sunday."

I mentally reviewed the calendar and allowed that this was correct.

"Yes, Sir."

"The Sabbath day."

I could have sworn, from my books, that that was Saturday, but I elected to agree with him and kept smiling: "Yes, Sir"

"I will be in church."

"What, all day?"

The old tumbledown ruin certainly wasn't my idea of a pleasant place to pass the time, but tastes, after all, did differ, and I supposed that a man who would actively request a tour of the Island's grisly stonework must have something of a fondness for the macabre.

"Oh no, just for the morning and evening services"

I stared at him blankly through the fog. It was on the tip of my tongue to say: "So you won't be wanting any beer then?" but something told me the this was the wrong answer. Besides, the Inn didn't even do a morning service.

"I do hope I shall see you there?"

He wanted to see me at the church? Was this an assignation? Had I missed something? Was this another of those things that I was just supposed to *know*?"

I pushed gamely through my bewilderment: "Of course, Sir…um, when should I…"

But he was beaming at me again, his usual diffidence replaced with a sudden practiced confidence.

"Morning service is from eight till ten, and evening is from seven till eight-thirty, but I'll have the bells rung a little early to make sure everyone can attend on time. Prayer books will be provided, but you may wish to bring your own cushions as I can't seem to locate any hassocks, which reminds me -"

He broke off to gaze seriously into my eyes: "Do you think Tom could let me have some wine for the communion? It's just that I was only able to bring a couple of bottles with me, and I'm not sure that will be enough"

Light pierced my mental fog: I had read about something like this.

This was a *Reverend* thing.

The *Reverend* Norman Poltwhistle had been lured to the Island under guise of our needing a vicar and a vicar he intended to be.

And I, more fool me, had just agreed to go and watch.

Still, I supposed that whatever a church service entailed, anything that involved books and wine couldn't be all that bad.

I rallied my disordered thoughts enough to assure him that while sufficient wine might be a little hard to come by, I was sure Tom would be able to find him something suitable and that he should tell him from me to be sure it was the very best whatever-it-was that we had.

This done, I somehow managed to conduct him out of the laundry and point him in the general direction of the brewing sheds then bustled back to the cramped, murky room, closed the door behind me, and leaned against it to marshal my thoughts.

Well, mostly to marshal my thoughts. Some small part of me might also have wanted to forestall any further interruption, but I dismissed that part with annoyance.

I needed him to interrupt me. To interrupt me with passion and vigour.

I suppressed a shudder at the thought and, in the absence of any such interruption, turned my attention to the soapy, sodden masses before me.

Really I thought, surveying the slimy morass of garments, this was completely unreasonable. None of the romantic heroines or wicked seductresses in books ever had to wrestle with soggy sheets. Even on those rare occasions when the heroine was supposed to be a servant of some kind she still never had to worry about more than a little light gardening or decorative needlework between intervals of resisting her employer's unsuitable advances.

More fool her, I added grumpily, hauling the first load into the trough: a pile of wet woolies would probably have done a lot more to dampen his ardour than a few embroidered buttercups.

Of course, heroines of gentle birth never seemed to have heard of laundry at all.

Which was odd, really, when one considered how much time they tended to spend creeping down dusty passageways, fleeing over muddy heaths and fainting all over the place wearing only the thinnest and most ethereal of white dresses. One would have thought the grass stains at least would have deserved a mention.

Still, I thought, wringing out the linen with only a little more vigour than was really warranted, perhaps the novelists had a point. Laundry was no compliment to lovelorn looks.

With that frustrating thought I addressed myself firmly to the former.

8

I got the washing done eventually.

According to The Lady's Book Of Household Management (3rd ed.) I should then have spread my linens out "upon the nearby hedgerows or on fresh mown grass" to take advantage of the natural bleaching properties of the sun.

From which it could be deduced that wherever the eponymous lady lived there was a deal more sunshine, and much less mud than was to be found anywhere upon the Island. And presumably hedges not entirely made out of thorns, as well.

I hung it out on lines. All of it. Which took the best part of an hour.

By the time I was finished, what little sun we had was already bidding fair to disappear behind a thick bank of ominously black clouds, but I did not care: I was tired, I was bedraggled, I was sticky and my feet were muddy from hanging out the wash. The laundry could go hang for all I cared.

I needed a bath.

In the normal way of things I could have closed up the inn and pulled the bath in front of the fire in the taproom. Molly and I had taken plenty of baths that way, soaking comfortably before the crackling logs, surrounded, on rainy days, by great drifts of white linen that swung gently steaming from the beams as they dried.

Today however there was a guest in the Inn. Today, therefore, the taproom remained open, the laundry hung *outside*, and if I wanted a bath I would have to take it in my room like a lady.

If a lady was expected to drag the tub up our non-Euclidean staircase, heat and transport all the water and fill the bath for herself, that is.

It was another hour before the bath was anything that could be described as "full", and my arms and legs complained all the more from hurrying up and down with the heavy cans of water, but as I lowered myself into its warm embrace I could not have cared less.

Not because the hot water was a balm to my aching limbs, though oh it *was*, but because I had a plan, a plan as simple as it was scientific. I was going to lie here, wallowing in the wonderfully clean, warm water until Norman Poltwhistle came in. As he crossed the landing he would catch sight of me through the artfully half-open door, become overwhelmed with uncontrollable lust, and insist on ravishing me on the spot.

Or possibly on the bed, I amended: this particular spot being somewhat cramped for two and more than a trifle wet besides.

My reasoning in this case was, I considered, excellent.

Instead of relying on my own deductions and observations, flawed as they clearly could be, I instead based my method on the reports of several men who had, by their own declaration been incapable of resisting such an attack.

Whenever I heard tell of a girl being troubled by some man, or taken advantage of, the tale would invariably be followed by with "Of course, she might have known it would happen, going out like that," and a chorus of solemn tutting.

Indeed, I recalled the time Molly discovered her then swain - thereafter known as That Rotten Arsehole Ned Cowen- pressing young Bessie Ogle uncomfortably against a tree.

Moll had detached him from his prey by means of a boot to the inside of the knee, then held him down while Bessie got in a kick or two of her own, but even as he limped away he could already be heard plaintively inquiring as to just what she had expected, dressed like that.

Since Bessie's attire had been almost entirely indistinguishable from that of every other young woman, and a good deal longer and more concealing than my or Molly's own, I could only assume that either the difference had been too subtle for mere female eyes to discern, or else that every man on the Island spent his days in a near constant state of agonising, uncontrollable priapism.

Of course, Molly herself was something of a paradox, since according to this theory she should have been unable to move without every man in sight flinging himself at her.

Even more than they did usually, I mean.

Still the basic principles seemed sound: either men found the merest hint of female flesh an irresistible enticement, or they simply assumed, in face of all evidence to the contrary, that it must be an invitation.

There was, of course, a third possibility, which was that some people would take any excuse that they could get and if they couldn't find an excuse then they would invent one. In which case, I had to admit, there was perhaps just a very slight chance that the polite, reserved Norman Poltwhistle would catch one glimpse of my naked body and recoil in horrified embarrassment.

Fortunately the plan allowed for that too: I hadn't missed the way he'd flinched away from Molly on that first night after all. If it turned out that his reaction to my glistening nubile flesh was one of terror, then I had only press my advantage and I could scare him off the Island that way. Wasn't that why the Poet had come here, after all? Fleeing the attentions of an over-eager inamorata? If I couldn't drive the Vicar away with ghosts, perhaps I could frighten him off with my bosom instead. Norman Poltwhistle, haunted everywhere he went by my nipples, like a murdered woman's eyes in a gothic novel.

If I was a little uncomfortable about pressing myself upon a theoretically unwilling suitor I pushed these misgivings away: it might not be the best or most elegant of plans, but with only three days left I hadn't the time to care, just so long as it worked.

And of course a pleasant advantage of the last outcome was that I would not at any point be required to actually sleep with him.

At that moment, sliding into the blissfully warm tub, I didn't care how the plan worked out just so long as it *worked*.

Besides all that, I really did need a bath. For a while I simply wallowed in the hot water, letting its comforting heat sink into my bones and wash away the weariness of the day. I idled there, letting my mind drift pleasantly and breathing in the clean, unsullied steam and the sweet, subtle scent of the soap.

It was a really *good* piece of soap: not the rough lye I'd been using earlier. Not even the so-called "herbal" soap that my Gammer made from ivy and which raised a blisteringly scarlet rash on the skin of anyone fool enough to use it.

This was luxurious soap: fine milled and creamy and smelling of something expensively exotic. As I slid its smooth, melting surface along my skin I felt sensuous and hedonistic. Which made sense when one considered that I had pinched it from the Poet's wash-stand when he left.

Well, there had to be *some* advantage in being the only one who ever did any work around here.

Now, breathing in that subtle but heady perfume, I imagined myself as one of the Poet's sensual beauties.

I stretched my arms extravagantly wide and let my head fall back as if in the throes of ecstasy. My hair, no longer heavy with wash-water, floated in a magnificent aureole about my head and brushed the smooth wooden boards beneath the tub. It was lucky those boards had been swept recently, I thought. After all, we seductresses must consider these things.

I was a magnificent goddess, wanton and alluring, irresistible to all who beheld me. I lay there, poised for discovery by the soon-to-be-stunned Reverend, and revelled in the sensual abandon of the pose. For about five minutes. And then I got a crick in my neck.

I adjusted my position, resting my head upon one dainty hand and gazing mysteriously over the water under the great tumbling sweep of my hair.

The edge of the tub dug into my elbow.

Willing myself to endure the discomfort, I forced myself to

maintain the pose, my face a perfect mask of Sphinx-like intrigue.

I stuck *that* out for about thirty seconds, and then I gave up and tried again.

I rolled onto one shoulder and trailed my fingers suggestively over the water's surface.

I lay back with my head on my arm and one dimpled knee poking tantalisingly up from a drift of soap bubbles.

I rolled over onto my front, supporting my chin upon my folded hands and swinging my feet above me in a theoretically winsome and adorable fashion.

I gave up and flopped over again, disgorging an accidental wave onto the floorboards as I did so.

There had to be a pose that worked.

It was all very well to be somewhat less than seductive in the fog and swelter of the laundry. Nobody could have shown to advantage there.

If Helen of Troy had been found up to her elbows in Menelaus' grubby nightshirts, her face would not have launched so much as a rubber duck.

If fabled what's-her-name the Ethiopian princess whose beauty enraged the gods had been chained to a rocky spur *in a laundry*, the sea serpent would have turned up his nose at her and gone off in a huff. Although not before remembering a few things that he'd been meaning to put in the wash, it won't take a minute to fetch them, you don't mind do you, seeing as you're doing a load already?

Well, probably.

But here I was, disporting myself in my bedchamber, clear of skin and -by this time- clean of limb. You would think I would be able to make something of that, wouldn't you?

I sighed and reorganised myself once more.

Eventually I found a pose that worked. I reclined on one hip, my knee pressed into the bottom of the tub, and one foot gripped firmly against the side wall. My arms were folded behind me, head pillowed on my hands and the great coiled mass of my hair. I gazed towards the door in what I hoped might be construed as a sultry, rather than a sulky fashion and awaited my despoiler.

I waited.

And I waited.

I developed an insistent sort of tickle in my nose, but still I waited.

I gave in, dealt with the tickle, repositioned myself, tried and failed to assume the same expression as before, and I waited.

I mentally ran through four different scenarios for my eventual discovery and subsequent ravishment, another four in which my abandoned ways drove him to immediate flight, and two more in which I lost my nerve and ran away, and still I waited.

I wondered whether he had somehow come in without me noticing, slipping up the stairs while my head was underwater, perhaps, and was even now sitting comfortably in his room, having completely failed to see me.

But that was just silly.

Or was it?

Perhaps...

There was a peephole from our room into his. Or rather, I should say, from his room into ours.

It had been put there by an overnight traveller who had been so struck by Molly's charms he decided that he needed a better view of them. Fortunately the sound of surreptitious drilling had alerted us both and once the hole was finished...Well, it turns out that a hole big enough to comfortably see through is also just big enough to admit one of Molly's dainty fingers. Tipped with Molly's dainty nail. At speed.

The man had left the next morning, in some haste, trying all the while to pretend that there was nothing at all unusual about the lumpish mass of bandages swathed around half his head. But the peephole remained.

I heaved myself out of the tub, dripped across to Molly's side of the room and cautiously pressed my eye to the hole. The room was empty.

Or rather, the space directly in front of the peephole was empty. The rest of the room could have been full to the gills and I wouldn't have had the faintest idea.

Maybe he was sitting right next to it?

No, now I was definitely over-thinking things.

I shook myself, accidentally spattering Molly's flowered coverlet with soapsuds, and slithered back to the bath, took up the pose, and waited.

Any moment now.

Any moment.

He was going to walk up those stairs, pass my open door, glance automatically in and…

Any moment now.

Finally, unable to sustain the sense of anticipation any longer I allowed myself to relax into the pose, sinking gradually lower in the consoling warmth and letting my eyelids slide gratefully closed, settling comfortably into the water even as I listened warily for Norman Poltwhistle's step upon the stair.

Of course I fell asleep.

I woke, hours later to find the bathwater cold, my limbs numb and nerveless, my fingers wrinkled with long soaking, and the sky outside inescapably, uncompromisingly black.

As I staggered out of the tub on legs that no longer remembered how to work, I noticed three things.

First, Molly had been in at some point, for the door was now closed and a thick towel hung over the side of the bed, over the optimistically turned back quilt.

Second, it had begun to rain.

And third?

There was no sign whatsoever of Norman Poltwhistle.

I checked, of course: pressing my eye to the spy hole then, seeing nothing but more darkness, turning my head to listen instead. Nothing. Not so much as a breath or the creak of a bedrope. Which was hardly conclusive evidence, admittedly, but there was an odd sense of absence, too: the sort of quiet found only when one is truly alone. The tiptoeing, breath-holding hush of an empty room.

I stood up, stretching my stiff limbs, and absently flipping Molly's pillow over to hide the drips. I would achieve nothing helpful maundering over a hole in the plaster. The Reverend could be anywhere by now, and even the most adventurous of heroines would only need to glance at the rainwashed blackness outside to decide that right now bed was the better part of valour.

Which is how I knew said heroines had servants. Or were blessed with a narrative that ignored such minutiae. For the rest of us it is a sad fact that, once a hot bath has eased all the aches and pains incurred in filling it, one needs must obtain a new set by emptying it out again.

I cast a longing glance at my bed. It sat there, soft, warm and inviting, and gloated at me. I ignored it. Perhaps a little more emphatically than was sensible given that my audience was a blanket-topped lump of wood. Well never mind: I was alone in my room, weighed down with cares and facing a wet and miserable task. If I wanted to snub the furniture I ruddy well could.

I firmly turned my back on the bed. Then I had to turn round again to twitch my clean shift from its foot and fumble my old leather slippers out from beneath it. Finally, averting my eyes and doing my best to communicate through action that the bed was far from forgiven for its rudeness, I added a heavy shawl over my wet hair and shoulders, scooped a bucketful of grimy bathwater, and staggered down the stairs.

It was chilly work and would have been even if I weren't already steeped in long-cooled bath water. I made my way through the Inn-yard, slipping and sliding on the wet cobbles and clawing my way past the clinging, waterlogged limbs of the still-hanging laundry, backed carefully through the gate, and dumped out the water into the already furiously swirling channel that ran alongside the lane. Then I slithered back up and did it again. And again. And again. And I was just lugging along a fifth sloshing bucketload when I noticed a tall figure half hidden behind a tree where the lane turned down the hill.

Actually.

Make that two figures.

My heart caught in my mouth: the first form was tall and angular, face and form obscured by a hat and long coat. The other was a little smaller, slighter - a woman perhaps?

I dropped the bucket in shock, water slopping against my calves and splashing over the stones. Could it be? Was this an assignation? Had the blessed, oblivious Reverend Norman Poltwhistle found his own solution to my problems? *And if so,* asked an unhelpful, impractical corner of my mind; *just what did she have that I didn't?*

The slightest idea of what she was doing, probably.

I crept closer. I'd get as near as I dared, see if I could get a better sense of what they were up to and then, well, if it was an assignation I had only to bide my time before loudly "discovering" them at some suitably importunate moment, and if it was just a chaste tryst in the almost-moonlight then at least I would be able to identify his light o' love and could be ready to give their romance a few solid nudges and hurry the whole thing along a little.

I slunk in a careful crouch along the low wall, coming to a halt in a stand of prickly bushes and realising, now that it was too late to do anything about it, that I should have brought along the bucket, by way of an alibi.

What would I say if I was challenged now? "*Just out for a walk, your reverence. Nice night isn't it?*" Well, if you liked unremitting rain I supposed it was. Or maybe "*Who, Sir? Me, Sir? Why I'm just emptying out the wash water. A woman's work is never done, you know. My bucket? I must have left it in the Innyard. Forget my own head next!*" No. Even Norman Poltwhistle might be hard-pressed to accept that. Perhaps I should sneak back and grab the thing.

No. If he challenged me I could damn well challenge him back. *I* wasn't the one having secret assignations under lonely trees in the middle of the night when all God-fearing people should be huddled in their beds.

I pushed a face-full of twigs out the way and looked determinedly upon the Reverend and his beloved.

Only it wasn't the Reverend.

It was Netta Stanley.

She didn't notice me, which was just as well, since if she had done I'd have needed to explain not just why I was standing in a bush, in the dark, in my nightdress, in the rain, but also why my mouth was hanging open and my eyes staring out of their sockets. I suspect, in fact, that if pressed I would very likely have been unable to offer very much of a response at all beyond "You...why?" or possibly "What?"

It's these little details that always trip one up.

So when no one so much as glanced in my direction I should have been relieved. Unfortunately I was far too busy wondering exactly what on the God's squelchy Isle was going on to draw the slightest grain of comfort from my apparent invisibility.

Why was Netta Stanley having a secret meeting, in the middle of the night, on the lane outside the Inn? I assumed it was a secret meeting, anyway, for her companion was swathed from head to toe in a long, black, hooded cloak of the kind that instantly draws attention to the underhanded, stealthy behaviour of its wearer, but it was always possible that they were just wearing it to keep off the rain.

It was possible, in fact, that it wasn't any sort of meeting, secret or otherwise: perhaps whoever it was was just out, enjoying a stroll in the admittedly awful evening weather when they ran into Netta on her way to... where would she be going? For that matter, where could she be coming from? Miser Farm was miles off in the wrong direction, and it was too late and far too wet to be coming back from a visit even if there were anywhere near here to have been visiting. There wasn't mind you. Indeed the only place within any reasonable sort of distance was the Inn.

Could they have been at the Inn? Netta had been in that afternoon, after all, though it was unlike her to stay away from her work even that long, let alone to linger late into the night. Still, perhaps she had just run into a friend at closing time and they had somehow kept talking. For hours. In the dark. And the rain.

As theories went this was palpably ridiculous but I didn't see any reason to stand around worrying about it now. Netta could look after herself. I quietly disentangled myself and began to back out of the bush.

Which was a shame. Because if I'd stayed a moment longer I might have heard more of what they were saying, or at least been able to tell who was saying it. As it was, the hiss and rattle of the rain filled the scant space between us swallowing up nearly all over sounds so that all I caught was "Trying to prevent the sacrifice" in a whisper so hoarse it could have come from almost anybody.

I froze on the spot. Not because the words had chilled me to the bone - I was already chilled thank you very much - but because they had been hoarsely whispered to Netta Stanley. And Netta shouldn't know anything about the sacrifices at all.

I craned forward again, scratching my cheek against the branches as I strained to listen. It was no use: with a good yard between us and the rain sleeting all around, even the most forceful stage-whispers would have been lost to the hissing clattering downpour.

Had I misheard? I had sacrifices on the brain just now, it was true. I tried to recall the shape of the words, the weight and measure of them, to fit some other, innocent phrase into the space they had taken up. "Standing here we're as cold as ice" perhaps, or "In here are a lot of mice"? Who knew what might be inside that cloak, after all? But nothing rang true, try as I might.

Whatever they were talking about it was coming to an end now: Netta was pulling aside branches, re-setting her practical felt hat to shield her from the rain, helping her companion out from beneath the sheltering boughs. I willed myself to stillness as they passed, holding my breath, heart hammering so fiercely it drowned out the thundering rain. Surely one or the other of them must see me. But they didn't. Instead they headed off toward the lane, then stopped suddenly, as the black cloaked figure seemed to catch imploringly at Netta's sleeve.

She shook her head firmly, leaning down to whisper into a hooded ear then, so near now that I could see every line and freckle on her face, she wheeled to look in the direction of the Inn: "You needn't worry," her words rang clearly through the rain; "*she* doesn't suspect a thing, I promise." And with an odd, secretive smile she was gone, loping down the lane, her accomplice's cloak streaming after her, to be swallowed up by the night.

Finally I dared to breathe again. No longer fearing discovery I was free to get myself out of the bush and back to the warmth and security of the Inn. Of course I didn't. I was too busy staring into the space Netta had left, eyes unseeing, my mind rushing in a thousand directions at once as I stood, my feet locked, frozen into place.

She? She who? Suspect what? Did she mean me? Suspecting something about the sacrifice? Logically speaking I could think of nothing else she could mean, but, *Netta*? How did she know what was going on? How could she know what I was up to? How, in ungrammatical short, did she know there *was* any up for me to be to? None of it made any sense, that sentence least of all.

I went to sit down in shock, then lurched back to my feet just in time as I remembered where I was. Right: muddy lane, dark, bush, rain. Nowhere to sit. Better panic standing up instead. I did so, pacing back and forth in the sludge as my nerves boiled to a peak.

After some time I had to acknowledge that panic wasn't helping and, since there was no-one there to snap me out of it I did so myself, aided by the rain which was better than a cup of water in the face, any day.

Having abandoned panic as a tactic I attempted rational deduction instead: Netta somehow knew about the sacrifices, Netta had a secret meeting with an unknown associate at dead of night, Netta had promised that someone - *I?* - did not suspect anything. All of which meant...what?

If only I knew who was under the hooded cloak I might have had some idea of what was going on, but as it was I was lost, foundering in confusion.

I mentally assigned different figures to the role. Perhaps it was Tom, secretly buying some new ingredient for an experimental ale? They were by the Inn, after all, and there wasn't much Tom wouldn't do in the name of better beer. But then Tom never wore hoods, or hats of any kind, and besides if they were going to meet why not do it in the relative comfort of the brewing sheds or even in the actual comfort of the Inn itself?

Or what about the Reverend, who had to be somewhere around, perhaps performing some sort of good work or act of Christian charity, with the hooded cloak to protect his clothes from the damp.

This idea rang even less true than the first, not only because the figure had been shorter than Norman Poltwhistle and the cloak considerably less suited to the rain than his usual heavy coat, but because whoever it was had seemed to move with an easy grace that was about as far as one could get from the flapping, flailing gait of a skidding flamingo with which that gentleman moved through the fair. Besides, Netta had always resisted charity of any kind, even when anyone had anything to give or the inclination to give it. I could think of any number of people more likely to be the recipients of the Reverend's kindness than Netta, and not one of them would have needed to stand on a rainy hillside to do it.

No, it wasn't the Reverend. But who could it be? Who would have either cause or the desire to wrap theirself in a cloak that all but screamed I Am Up To No Good and hold a secret meeting at dead of night?

The obvious answer, of course, was Himself With The Apple Trees. Mind you, Himself wouldn't have needed to actually be conspiring at anything in order to do that: he quite regularly showed up at the Inn to skulk in the shadows with an enigmatic look upon his stern, saturnine countenance, and it almost never amounted to anything. Himself would be just the sort to accidentally spill the beans about the sacrifice, too, being of the opinion that it was no use having a secret unless everyone could see that you had it, and that being the case, one might expect Netta to accept this revelation with equanimity, just as one did all the rest of the twaddle the self-styled Master of Arts Arcane liked to spout. Indeed, if it was Himself then I had nothing to worry about at all.

Of course this theory ignored the fact that Himself was far too tall to fit under the cloak, as well as the fact that he was very nearly the least likely person to have any sort of dealings with anyone as determinedly practical as Netta Stanley.

He might have known her before of course: they were both from the mainland after all and it was well known that Netta had come here fleeing a life that was somehow much much worse than the one she'd made for herself. Perhaps he'd known her there, had arranged her arrival for some nefarious scheme or other then…had nothing whatsoever to do with her for four years before suddenly setting her to watch over the Inn just in case one of the barmaids took it into her head to somehow prevent the sacrifice?

I could see Himself plotting something like that, stupid as it was. Actually, I could see him relishing it, gazing gleefully over his steepled fingers as he admired its convoluted complexity. The difficulty was, I couldn't see Netta going along with it, even in the name of humouring the idiot.

Of course, she might not have had a choice. Never mind pie in the sky nonsense about engineering her escape, what if he had just recognised her, vaguely, as someone he'd seen somewhere, and had taken steps to learn who she was? I could almost see him, plying Old Man Morris with ale, listening with a face of all-knowing wisdom as the old man rambled his way proudly through the whole sad tale. And then, having gloated his fill over a secret everyone on the Island already knew, going to her and saying: what? "Work for me or I'll write to your husband"?

Was Netta Stanley being blackmailed?

It made a horrible sort of sense. Himself would no doubt revel in the manipulative wickedness of it all, without a thought for the real life that he could ruin, and Netta... Netta who'd ditched her silks and pearls to labour day in and day out come rain or pitiless sun, who never spoke a word of the life she'd had before, never complained no matter how hard the work, who kept herself so determinedly to herself... I didn't know what she'd escaped, but I wondered what she wouldn't do to keep from going back to it. Joining in one of Himself's nonsensical schemes must have seemed a small thing in comparison.

A small thing for her. But it could be the difference between life and death for Norman Poltwhistle.

I had to remember that. I couldn't let myself be dragged down by my pity for poor, hard-working Netta Stanley, escaping from the God knew what. But it was hard, so very hard not to feel sympathy for the fragile, silk-clad girl who had become the spare, hardworn woman with calloused hands and rough, men's clothes upon her back. It was agonisingly hard, but still, I had to do it: the bonfire was less than three days away and there simply wasn't time to care about them both.

I'll save him first, I promised myself, *and then I'll save her*. Somehow. If she even needed saving.

I shook myself crossly: this was all nonsense. Oh, without a doubt I could see Himself coming up with a stupid plan like that. I could see him carrying it out, too. I could certainly see him hunching down under the cloak to play the blackmailer, hissing his commands in a throaty rasp, believing himself the very master of disguise. What I couldn't see was him getting to the end of that little scene under the tree without flinging off the cloak, drawing himself up to his full, looming height and making sure Netta knew exactly who was the devious mastermind behind her tragic undoing. No it wasn't the Apple-Witted Lord, that much was sure.

Besides, that last whisper hadn't looked like a hunted woman addressing her blackmailer: there had been something gentle about it, almost tender, I would have said she was more protective than needing to be protected.

Whoever was under the cloak, it wasn't someone to be afraid of, then. An accomplice or a supplicant, rather than an aggressor.

Still, they had definitely been talking about the sacrifice. Probably. No, almost certainly. So why would an unspecified Islander have been talking to someone who shouldn't even know about the sacrifices, in secret, at dead of night?

Perhaps they weren't worried that someone was going to prevent the sacrifice. Perhaps someone else was trying to prevent it. Perhaps they had confided their fears to the one person they knew had nothing whatsoever invested in the bonfire. *Perhaps* Netta Stanley was planning to disqualify the Reverend herself.

Mind you, if I had to name the person on the Island least likely to figure as a seductress then, well, Netta would definitely be my second choice. After myself.

I shook my head angrily to clear it.

There was no point to any of this. I didn't know anything. All I had to go on was a handful of words and a somewhat suspicious encounter, and here I stood, in the rain, making up stories. Maybe Netta was embroiled in some awful plot, or maybe she was an unwitting tool, or someone's faithful servant or their victim or the instrument of their undoing. Maybe she was engaged in a torrid affair, for that matter, or perhaps she was the blackmailer, or maybe they just happened to run into one another while they were both out picking ruddy mushrooms. I didn't know, I couldn't know, and I wouldn't get anywhere by standing here becoming one with the shrubbery. I stomped angrily back to the bucket and picked it up. This was why heroines didn't go out on rainy nights: they knew that was where the plot was.

I trudged back through the yard and slipped miserably up the stairs. The bath was still half-full, but I was, by now, so wet, so cold, and so impossibly weary that I simply couldn't force myself to fill the bucket again. I abandoned it by the fireplace, exchanged my drenched and muddied shift for a cleaner one, wrung out my hair, and slithered gratefully between the sheets.

I had enough to worry about as it was.

But I might just keep an eye on Netta, all the same.

9

I did not sleep well that night.

To begin with, I was chilled through from lying for goodness knows how long in the cooling water and then spending a further unspecified amount of time, lurking in the lane in my underthings. On top of this, it was all very well to tell myself to stop thinking about Netta Stanley, but as soon as I made any real effort to prevent myself from thinking of her I found myself, perforce, thinking about not thinking about her, which led to thinking about her, which was no help whatsoever. I tried thinking about the Reverend instead, but that only made things worse, as my various frettings and perturbations warred with one another for supremacy, then ganged up together to give me a headache.

I curled into a shivering ball and waited for sleep to overcome me.

Sleep, much like the dear Reverend, failed to cooperate.

The cold was bone deep, and clung to me in exactly the way one Norman Poltwhistle hadn't yet, refusing to disappear, even in my usually cosy nest of blankets.

On top of this there was no escaping the fact that I had already slept that night. Perhaps it had not been for as long as I needed, or as comfortably, but the well-trained habit of my body insisted that I had slept, and I had woken up, and now it was time to get on with the day.

Perhaps I should finish emptying the bath out after all? No. I firmly ignored my shivers, my insistent wakefulness, and every nagging prickle of my industrious conscience, and told myself to sleep.

This worked precisely as well as you would expect.

I turned over, pressing my face into my pillow: *go to* sleep *you idiot. You're cold and tired and overwrought,* I told myself, *so get some sleep and in the morning you won't be.*

You've got a long and probably frustrating day ahead of you and nothing to do now but sleep, so by the ichor-crusted claws of the Island God Go. To. Sleep.

For some reason this also failed to help.

It did, however, distract me from my woebegone shudderings. By making me fret over tomorrow instead.

What was one supposed to do in a church? Was I about to make an utter idiot of myself?

Again, whispered the unhelpful part of my subconscious.

Would *anyone* know what to do? Would anyone but me even turn up? Would my beloved countrymen not only *not* turn up to the church but, whipped into a religious fervour by the upcoming festivities, decide that this was the perfect time to try burning it down again? Would the services really take up the whole day? And if they did, how on the God's muddy Earth was I supposed to save a man's life with only two days left in which to do it?

Especially with Netta's nebulous plot in the background, boding ill at me.

Even more especially when the man in question seemed completely uninterested in seducing or in being seduced.

Or was he?

Perhaps that was why he hadn't come in yet. Perhaps he was even now in some bedchamber or other, his hands caressing some theoretically nubile form, lithe, and naked and...I shuddered at the thought.

Still, I reasoned, that would certainly solve the problem wouldn't it?

Always supposing he wasn't too much of a gentleman to tell anyone. Which he almost certainly was.

And finally, musing over whether I ought to be relieved or

insulted if someone had succeeded where I so clearly failed, whether there could really be anyone desperate enough to find a face like a half-plucked chicken attractive, and whether it really was possible to be too polite to live, I began to drift off to sleep at last.

So that, of course, was when Norman Poltwhistle finally came in.

At once I was awake again, asking myself where he had been, who he was with, what they had been doing.

Was he disqualified as a sacrifice? Was he not?

Was he doomed anyway simply because he had no idea there was anything to be disqualified from?

Should I go and *ask*?

Should I, if I was getting up anyway, go and empty out the rest of the bathwater before somebody had an accident?

I pulled the quilt over my head and tried, frantically, to think of absolutely anything else.

Three hours later, as the first glimmers of morning began to whisper over the sill, I finally fell asleep. And was immediately woken by Molly, creeping into the room and falling over the bath.

Knowing that there was, at this point, no point at all in going back to sleep, I naturally wanted nothing more in the world than to huddle under my now voluptuously warm blankets and hide from reality.

Comfort warred briefly with common sense, and lost, as it was depressingly wont to do.

Pulling on my clothes in the half-light, I tiptoed past Molly's already delicately snoring form and out into the inn.

I sulked my way through the morning's chores with all the fervour of one who knows they are being worthily diligent but who doesn't have to like it.

Pint pots shuddered on their shelves. Spiders fled before the furious broom. Kindling leapt into frightened life at a spark from my fingers. I swept out into the inn-yard and was promptly pecked on the ankle.

That cockerel has no sense for the dramatic.

By the time it had begun to really look like morning the chickens were fed, water was drawn, the bread was put in to rise, and the porridge was singing smugly over the fire. I set out bowls for everyone, including Tom who had, for a wonder, not fallen asleep in the shed last night, and sat, blowing gracelessly on my own portion and contemplating the invigorating effect of a thoroughly bad mood.

According to everything I had read on the subject, one was supposed to do no work on the Sabbath. *Or,* the pedant in me added, *on a Sunday.*

Exactly how one was meant to achieve this had always baffled me, but now I suspected I had the answer: the writers of those books simply slept luxuriously through the early hours while their unappreciated servants swept through a mountain of labours under the spurring influence of social inequality.

I wasn't entirely sure how they rationalised the appearance of all the enormous Sunday dinners which are so frequently a feature of such books, but I supposed a mind that could believe that floors swept and fires kindled themselves would be capable of overlooking almost anything.

A creak from the stairs interrupted my musing.

I looked up to see Norman Poltwhistle in what I assumed must be his full clerical regalia, descending into the common room with the magisterial dignity of a half-hatched chick.

As he approached the table I considered my strategy.

By rights I should say something flirtatious at this point.

For once my thoughts were not on the seduction at hand: bantering with the customers was simply what one did. It couldn't be anything too flowery of course, but a nicely turned compliment such as "My, my, don't you scrub up nice?" was generally considered de rigeur for situations such as this.

One could, of course, take things further if one was so inclined: a little deniable innuendo was never out of place or, if one had the wit for it, one might utter something just sharp enough to sting the pride without straying into the realm of outright insult.

That last was always particularly successful if you could pull it off: the customer always felt compelled to answer so one could, with a little work, keep up a back and forth that would last a good five minutes and end with the target feeling remarkably clever. And then he would buy more beer.

I doubted that any amount of repartee would induce the sober Reverend to spontaneously purchase a pot, much less drink it, but still, honour required that I try.

I considered my quarry.

He was swathed in some sort of billowy, black drapery which had much the same effect as his habitual greatcoat did, although this at least seemed to flap rather less, and went some way toward softening the effect of his elbows. About his neck he wore stark bands of stiff white linen, on which his head sat like a badly coiffed egg on a plate.

It wasn't the worst robe I had ever seen.

The Island Faith doesn't have an official costume for ceremonial occasions, so attire ran the gamut from grubby smocks through to ostentatious robes.

His was at least better than the flowing white muslin affected by Himself With All The Apple Trees, at the last tragically victimless bonfire. This had puffed up in the wind until he looked like an over inflated marshmallow, before catching some stray sparks and going up in a blaze that had got everyone quite excited before he managed to tear it off.

His saturnine eyebrows still weren't completely recovered.

Compared to that the sacerdotal robes of the Reverend Poltwhistle were a pillar of restraint and practicality.

Still, what could I say?

You look marginally less ridiculous than usual? No.

Congratulations! Your ceremonial gown looks slightly less absurd than the one belonging to one of the people who are plotting to roast you alive? Emphatically not.

"Would you like to borrow a comb?" No, no, that was the worst of all.

Wait. Had I just...

"Oh, thank you Dora, no: I have one of course, but I'm afraid there's no doing anything with it" he waved airily headwards as he pulled out his seat.

Yes, it seemed I had indeed said that out loud.

"Oh, I don't know Sir, I think it suits you somehow" I recovered, mendaciously.

"Really?" he looked surprised, "My man always says I look like a parrot in a thunderstorm"

"Your...*man*, Sir?" I tried to quell my excitement: this would be the perfect solution, if he was already in a relationship with a man then *of course* he would have been disqualified by now.

All I had to do was let the bad news slip to a cherished customer or twelve and then...

"Yes, my valet, Cecil. My gentleman's gentleman, you know"

Excitement quelled itself extempore.

I did know.

While it was true that the only "gentleman's gentleman" in these parts was Mister Wyndham who had used to keep company with a *very* fine young man, I had read enough to understand what the term usually implied.

The right Reverend Norman Middlename Poltwhistle was almost certainly *not* schtupping his valet.

"...but he's visiting his people inland at the moment, and I just don't have his touch with the pomatum".

I mumbled sympathetically around the last of my porridge and pushed back my chair.

"Still, he'll be here in a few days now, and I shall just have to muddle through -oh, are you going?"

"Yes, sorry, I just remembered some work that needs," *damn! Sunday!* "needs leaving alone, so I'm just going to go and make sure nobody does it. Enjoy your breakfast, Sir."

And I fled, intemperate up the stairs.

Barmaid's honour be damned: I could not engage in flirtatious banter about his valet.

Having nothing better to do with myself I decided to wake everyone else up as well.

If nothing else they could shield me from manservant-related repartee. And anyway, their porridge was going cold.

There was no answer when I knocked at Tom's door, but I could hear him moving around inside, so I let him know that breakfast was downstairs if he should want any, and went to see if Molly was awake. She, having had enough of early rising and virtuous labour yesterday, was sprawled face down on her bed, snortling into her pillow. I sat on the end of the bed and prodded her toes till she woke, then banished her downstairs with the promise of breakfast and the questionable pleasures of church still to come.

This accomplished, I lurked haplessly on the window-ledge, idly bailing out the bath tub into the puddled yard below.

I honestly wasn't aiming at the cockerel, and really the wretched beast should have had more sense than to be stalking about in the rain anyway, but it was remarkable how many of my innocent sallies seemed to land square on his silly, smug crest. I was just leaning out a little further, and musing that if he moved just a quarter of an inch to the left then this next one would catch him right in the tail feathers, when the inn door opened and a taller, darker, but equally ridiculous form stepped down into the yard.

Restraining myself just in time, I regained my grip on the water-can and watched in bemusement as the good Reverend crouched and fussed over the dripping cockerel as though it were a treasured family pet.

I expected to see him go down under a furious assault of beak and spur, but instead the contrary bird responded to his cosseting with a show of preening and posing that made me wish I hadn't put down the can.

I suppose he recognised one of his own.

Once the stupid cock had been thoroughly lavished with attention, his attendant seemed to recollect that there were other purposes in his life than pandering to poultry, drew himself up, and billowed out of yard like a small but well meaning stormcloud.

That probably meant that it was time for church.

Downstairs I was surprised to find that not only was Molly eagerly waiting, arrayed in her best holiday bodice and with a petticoat a good three inches longer than was her usual wont, but Tom too had resisted the lure of the brewing sheds in favour of digging out his good, soft coat and a battered felt hat that I suspected of dating back to his grandfather's day.

He noticed me looking and glanced down uncomfortably.

I redirected my gaze hastily but: "Tom. You've got a hat!"

"I have." He seemed somewhat proud of this fact.

"But you don't wear hats." It was true. He never did. He didn't like the way the band felt round his head, or the way the shadows got in his eyes. In all the time I had known him, even on the very brightest, sunniest days, he had never once worn a hat.

"Vicar says you have to have hats for church."

This might be true, but all the same: "Are you going to *wear* it?"

"No," He gave a smile. "Men take their hats off inside, Vicar said. He was most particular about that. Women wear their hats inside and men take them off. Wanted to be sure to let us know. So I don't need to wear it. I can just carry it."

I supposed it had been kind of him to tell us. He must have worried that we wouldn't know what to do, after so long, or perhaps I'd given things away a little with my confused blithering yesterday - but honestly, you try thinking quickly when you're up to your ears in steam and dirty water. It was kind too to reassure Tom that he wouldn't have to actually *wear* the hat.

"I've got one for you as well." Tom reached behind him and withdrew…a *thing*.

It looked like a broad wicker basket with no handle, turned upside down and with several improbably pink feather plumes fastened to one side. There was a cascade of ribbons - also pink - trailing down on the same side, with matching bows holding up a frill of lace under what was presumably the brim, and yet more ribbons to tie the whole thing on with. He must have got it from the lost property box.

"I can't wear that!" I said; "I'll look like a demented mushroom".

"You have to have a hat for church." said Tom; "Look, Molly's got one too."

Molly's hat, which I did indeed recognise as having been left behind by an overnight visitor, was a dainty scrap of silk, designed to sit neatly over one ear, finished with a spray of artificial flowers and a wisp of gauze. I could see just by looking at it that it would set her off to perfection. Mind you, so would just about anything.

Meanwhile… "You said women wear their hats inside," I argued desperately; "so I don't need to wear it going there. I can just carry it, and put it on when I go in."

"Alright," agreed Tom; "but don't forget it mind."

I promised hastily that I wouldn't and looked frantically for a distraction: "You said the Vicar told you about the hats?"

"That's right," Tom repeated "Hats on for women, and hats off for men".

I wondered what you were supposed to do if you weren't either. There had to be a rule, I supposed: they wouldn't go making complicated, hat-based rules of etiquette for two genders, and completely forget about all the rest. That would just be silly. There was probably some other variation he hadn't bothered to mention. Perhaps a hood, or a scarf of some kind, or… or perhaps I should get away from the subject of hats before I wound up actually wearing one: "Did you talk about anything else interesting?"

Tom thought about this: "Beer." He said eventually.

"Just beer?" It was quite possible: beer was Tom's favourite topic of conversation and he could spend hours, with the right person, expounding on every aspect, from selecting the right hops, to the best temperature at which to drink each and every sort. Of course, that would depend on Norman Poltwhistle somehow being the right kind of person. If he was, it was a mark in his favour.

"It's not that Tom's bad with people," Molly had observed, once; "it's that *people* are bad at *Tom*." She had a point.

"And his uncle," Tom added, after a moment.

"His uncle?" I was slightly nonplussed by this sudden change of subject.

"Yes," Tom answered definitely; "Very important man, he said. Worries about him. Only relative you see. Sent him here to…" he tailed off uncertainly. "Don't think he said why he sent him," he added thoughtfully; "Said a lot of things mind, but I don't think they meant anything."

He paused for a minute.

"Said "um" a lot, too. Probably didn't want to tell me." He concluded, seeming perfectly content with this unsatisfactory state of affairs.

"Doesn't like beer." He added, suddenly.

"Who, Norman?"

"No, his uncle. How we got onto the subject. Don't think your Reverend dislikes beer." I knew better but declined to comment; "Asked for that, specially: beer not wine."

And he pointed to a small barrel sitting at his feet.

"Promised him I'd deliver it this morning."

He considered for a moment then added "Sensible fellow, I call him."

I declined to give my own opinion on the matter, but covered my discomfiture by passing the awful hat to Molly and bending to give a hand with the barrel.

But really, I thought, seduction might not be enough any more.

If both Molly *and* Tom approved of him I might end by having to marry the man.

Beset by horrible visions of matrimony, I took a firm hold on the barrel and we headed out into the rain. Well, into the drizzle. The rain, it seemed, was beginning to die off, and apart from the mud, puddles, unexpected slippery stones, and the still wet and flapping laundry that caught at our arms and tried to entangle us as we passed, there was little to impede our progress on the way to the church.

This, of course, meant that my companions and I were free to turn our thoughts to idle chatter as we strolled down the lane.

Or rather that *Tom* and *Molly* were free to grill me about my supposed paramour.

What did he think of the Island? Was it different to where he came from? Was he glad he'd come now he'd met me? Was he terribly romantic? What did we talk about? Did he like books? Did he like the same books as me? Was he still doomed to a horrible fiery death? And did he prefer a pale ale or a milk stout?

I answered as best I could: that I couldn't know what he thought of our Island as he'd hardly insult it to my face; that I didn't know where he came from but it was probably less muddy -wasn't everywhere less muddy? that I supposed he wasn't *terrible* at romance; that we had talked about the sorts of things people usually talked about; that he certainly *owned* several books; that I had somehow failed to introduce the topics of overblown novels, esoteric sciences, horrible executions, or household management - with the exception of laundry - into the conversation so I had no idea what he thought of them; and that yes, yes he was thoroughly doomed, but I was *working on it*.

On the subject of beer I thought it best to withhold counsel.

By the time I had made it through all of that we were barely out of the inn yard and I was out of breath and blushing like a beacon fire.

Fortunately Molly took pity on me and asked Tom about the barrel we were carrying.

This, of course, took care of the rest of the journey, by the end of which I knew more about the preparation and proper storage of porter than I was ever likely to need in a full lifetime of barmaidry.

I also knew that this was, in fact, next week's barrel, to supplement the two that Tom had already set up last night, "But won't be worth nothing, that won't, with the sediment not settled right: you get along there next week and you'll find something worth trying."

I was strangely touched: Tom at least must have some faith in my abilities if he imagined there was still going to be a Vicar next week.

In this way our journey was enlivened until we rounded the corner by the church and came up against an enormous throng of people and a raucous clamouring of bells.

The bells were in the hands of three unusually shiny-faced urchins who I recognised vaguely as living down by the fishing fleet. They were swinging them with great joy and vigour, and absolutely no care for the safety of passers by.

Which, given the aforementioned throng, was something of a hazard.

This crowd was entirely occupied with trying to squeeze through the high, arched doorway of the church, while avoiding the chaotically flailing bells.

Of course, the problem with any sort of crowd is that it is made up of lots and lots of individual people, few of whom can see more than the particular bit of crowd that they are in. This should, in theory, result in a careful, slow moving, mass of people, each attentively watching out for their neighbour on the understanding that unless everyone works together then nobody will get anywhere. In practice it resulted in a chaotic scrum.

Larger people barged into smaller people, smaller people tried to squeeze between larger people. Tall people, taking advantage of their lofty vantage points, looked out for openings in the morass and lunged quickly toward them, only to trip over the smaller people on the way. Families with small children clung to one another in terror lest they be swept away in the current. Anyone who tried to dodge out of the way of assault by handbell stood a good chance of shoving someone else into it. And of course, wherever it looked as though someone might be able to find a safe way through, there would be two people, standing immovable, apparently unaware of the peril on every side and driving everyone else to distraction by *having a pleasant conversation.*

We looked upon the mayhem and decided we wanted none of it.

So while Tom sloped off around the side somewhere with his precious burden, Molly and I skirted the edges of the confusion, nipped over the low wall into the meagre churchyard, and squeezed neatly in through one of the unfinished walls at the back. Inside, the church had been transformed.

Well, no, it hadn't really, but it would be nice to think that it had.

The empty, grassy space had been filled with rows of benches set at regular intervals, with a clear path going down the middle.

I recognised some of the seats as long trestles from the Inn, and there was one battered settle that I suspected I had seen during my earlier excursions into the Rectory, but the rest were different: big, old things that the Reverend must have dragged out from goodness knows where. They shone in the dark space with the soft gleam of care and beeswax.

Candles, good candles of clean-burning white wax, had been fastened to the walls and along the ends of the benches, and massed on top of the tall, blockish altar at the front.

Behind this, and to the tall, wooden bookrest in front of it, great bundles of marram grass had been tied, corn dolly fashion, in the rough shape of a cross.

The whole thing, if one ignored the jostling, bickering crowd cramming into the benches at the front, gave one an almost indescribable sense of peace and tranquility.

So no, it wasn't a miraculous transformation, but it was an incredible amount of work for one man, and I felt it deserved my appreciation. In fact, I realised to my chagrin, it was so much work that it couldn't have left any time for illicit encounters with his female parishioners. This, no doubt, was where Norman had been last night. Drat it.

Well honestly, I scolded myself, *with all the fuss you made when you thought he'd been dallying with some random woman, you'd think you could muster at least a little relief at realising he hasn't.*

I couldn't.

There were two days till the sacrifice, and its prospective victim was still as innocent and unsullied as the day he came.

Two days to live, and instead of debauching himself in wicked dalliances, that blessed idiot had wasted his night on hard work and piety.

It was...it was...It was just *typical* was what it was.

Typical what I was not sure, but it was typical nonetheless.

It was possible, I reflected ruefully, that it was typical Norman Poltwhistle.

And that, when one came to consider it, was my difficulty in a nutshell.

I was jarred from my thoughts by a firm but dainty hand upon my elbow, and a hiss of "Dora, stop staring into nowhere like a duck stuck on a sandbar, and sit down!" And before I had time to wonder when I had become the peagoose moping about her ailing love affairs and left Molly to be the practical one, she had seized me by the arm and yanked me down into a seat.

I sat down with a bump and tried to reorient myself.

"Ah, Margaret...Theodora"

Molly's name is no more Margaret than mine is Theodora, but that was beside the point. The point being that she had sat us slap down next to Himself With The Apple Trees.

Practical one my foot.

My Lord With The Orchard turned his sinister gaze upon us and quirked one elegant eyebrow. "I do trust you are taking good care of our guest. I should so hate any...*harm* to come to him"

"Oh indeed Sir", I replied in my best Bucolic Conspirator, "He's safe as houses with us, never you fear"

The great advantage of talking to someone with an addiction to double meanings, is that you can speak nothing but the absolute candid truth and he will assume that he is being most awfully clever.

The Lord Of The Pippins smiled a chilling smile: "The good Reverend must think himself fortunate to be in the company of two such...*devout* young women".

Molly and I ducked our heads to obscure our modest blushes and incidentally to stifle a very immodest attack of the giggles.

Johnny Appleseed was not, strictly speaking, a native Islander.

His parents had come here, quite inexplicably, for their health when he was just a baby, building a picturesque house on the top of a cliff, and shielding it from the rough salt winds with a sprawling mass of apple trees.

Since apples like salt and hard weather only a little less than people do, these trees had never yet put out blossom, let alone fruit, but that hadn't prevented the old lord and lady from fussing over them with brushes and pruning knives and all manner of paraphernalia, just as though they knew what they were doing. Still, it kept them happy, and as they largely kept to themselves and didn't bother anyone, most of the time we Islanders had simply left them to it.

Their son was another matter.

His parents, as was usual for the Quality, had doted on him in his infancy, then packed him off to school as soon as he became large enough to be a nuisance. We had seen him from time to time, during the holidays, lurking in the branches as they worked, leering at passers by like some horrible little woodland spirit. But as time went by he spent more and more time away at his studies until finally he was barely even heard of.

And then his parents died and he came back from the university and, well, people had Hopes.

The man who returned was not the boy who had gone away: he was tall, elegantly formed, exquisitely dressed, and carried himself with a discernible air of superiority.

So superior, indeed, did he seem to consider himself, that you could hardly blame anyone for assuming he was a perfect candidate for the sacrificial fire. After all, even if he did condescend to fraternise with us peasants, what sensible person would ever touch him?

Several, as it turned out.

Even when the tales of his philandering started to spread a few Islanders were tempted to give him the benefit of the doubt, so to speak, and I must admit that after quite a short time in his presence even I had begun to see their point, but after the fourth tearful not-quite-a-maiden had confessed to her indiscretions it had to be acknowledged that the young gentleman was almost certainly *not* qualified. And then to put a cap on it all, young Janey Morris had turned up pregnant.

To give him his grudging due, Himself had done pretty well by Janey.
Of course he couldn't very well marry her, his sense of his own importance being what it was, but he made sure she was housed and supported, and did his best to supply all her needs.To his daughter he was a distant parent at best, but he provided for her handsomely enough, and acknowledged her proudly.

The poor child was named Belethoperis, at his insistence, and he referred to her at all times as "My *natural* daughter" in a way that he probably thought sounded excitingly dangerous and bohemian but which just gave one the impression that all of his other children were unspeakable horrors from beyond the veil, with eldritch tentacles and far too many teeth.

Belle's quite a nice girl, really, if a little too interested in bees.

When he turned up to that year's bonfire wearing a high collared robe of red velvet with astrological symbols embroidered on it in gold, it became clear that somehow his Lordship had got religion before religion could get him.

From that point on he had assumed the charge of all our rites and ceremonies.

Which is to stay that he assumed that he was in charge, and nobody bothered to disillusion him.

These days whenever there was a bonfire or a ritual of any kind he could be found, posing dramatically with his back to the light, declaiming some nonsense or other and declaring that "Surely the God will bless our works and the apples will return" just as if anyone had ever cared about his ruddy trees to begin with. He generally had a few impressionable young people hanging on his every word and trying to imitate his sinister smile, but they always grew out of it after a while, so mostly people just smiled politely and worked around him.

I lifted my eyes demurely and offered My Lord Of The Fruitless Endeavour a carefully conspiratorial smirk.

Then I turned my attention firmly to the front of the room, warding off any further significant ellipses.

The service was about to begin.

10

In a different sort of story I'm sure it would have been a beautiful scene.

Almost all the right elements were there: the earnest Vicar, a newcomer but determined to do good; the church that he had transformed through hard work and dedication; the sunlight slanting through the windows to fall like a benediction upon the heads of a congregation gathered together for the first time, and now prepared to raise their voices in jubilant song.

There were just two problems.

Firstly, most of said congregation were looking forward to said Vicar's grisly death.

And secondly, none of us knew the tune.

There was a brief, intensely uncomfortable silence as this sank in.

Everyone tried to avoid everyone else's gaze, while simultaneously glancing at their neighbour in the hope that they might somehow be doing something helpful. If eyes could be said to shuffle, these did.

Lips mumbled the words uncertainly, brief attempts at finding some sort of tune burst out intemperately here and there then stuttered into embarrassed silence. It was all quite agonisingly uncomfortable.

And then, in a rich, powerful baritone, The Master Of The Blighted Ruddy Arbours began to sing.

He sang with the certainty of one who had done so a thousand times before. He sang with verve, and conviction, and just a touch of patronising smugness. He sang with a confidence and assurance that swept everyone at the back of the church up in his wake.

Thanking our God that a university education was apparently good for *something*, we lifted our voices and joined in the song.

It was just a little unfortunate that he did this at precisely the same moment that the currently extremely Reverend Norman Poltwhistle did the exact same thing at the front of the church.

We were several verses in before anyone realised that what the Vicar was singing was not, in fact, the same tune as we were singing. At that point there wasn't very much point in stopping.

The same thing happened with the next song, and, after we had been welcomed on behalf of several people who didn't seem to have been able to make it today, with the song after that.

I could tell by the way he dramatised himself that the would be Lord of the Hesperides was now imagining the whole thing to be some sort of display of his power and dominion in the face of an interloper's god, but since Norman didn't seem to have noticed, I decided not to worry about it.

A few carefully sly glances in Himself's direction whenever he tried to catch my eye, and I was free to watch the room again.

It must be said that the service didn't really hold the attention of the congregation. A few people perked up when they were told they should be fishers of men, but once it became clear that this wasn't a reference to any kind of ritual drowning they lost interest again.

But of course they weren't really there for the service. They were there to see their lamb brought to the slaughter.

That was why they had pushed and jostled to get into the church, why they had fought and argued to get closer to the man in the pulpit.

It hadn't been a matter of mere curiosity at this newcomer amongst us, or any thought of sparing his feelings in the face of an empty church. It hadn't even been the need, as I had assumed, to keep up a pretence, to lull him into a sense of security and belonging.

No. All about the room people stared in avid glee at the gentle twit of a man who two mornings from now they would be happily burning to death.

I wondered why he couldn't see it: the hope in the posture of the most hopeless, the self-satisfaction of others, the horrible glee of those who had no real faith in any of it working, but who were looking forward to hearing the screams anyway.

Worst of all were the true believers. I saw them, dotted about the room, stern, and calm, and watchful, like cowmen keeping a firm hand upon a wilful calf.

I knew them, the way they talked in the bar at night, the way they went through their days, never changing, never faltering in what they knew was right. I knew the bitterness of talking with them, of taking a man through an argument, step by step, showing him the sense of every part of it, meticulously unweaving his counter-argument, providing proof upon proof for my every assertation, demonstrating the simple and irrefutable truth of my words, only to have it all slide away in the face of his unalterable belief in his own opinion. He'd a right to his opinion, hadn't he?

I knew the sneering half-laughter as I served his friends, days later in the bar, the contemptuous dismissal in their eyes. I knew their implacable certainty, the absolute immovability of their hearts. They made no pretence of devotion now, but watched him, their faces wooden and impassive, and somehow far more frightening than those who merely wanted to watch him burn.

And here and there, interspersed amongst the rest, were those who shifted uncomfortably upon their benches, who kept their heads turned down and would not meet the Reverend's eyes. I saw their discomfort, the guilt they felt, the shame at what they knew was to come. I suppose I should have felt a rush of fellow feeling for these few like minds in the crowd.

Mostly I despised them.

You fix it, I thought. *You make a fool of yourself talking about ancient gods and grisly sacrifices. You tell him to run, and if enough of you do it, maybe he'll listen. Or you sleep with him, save him that way so I don't have to. You can't make a worse job of it than I am.*

But I knew they wouldn't.

They were each of them, so far as they knew, alone with their conscience and they would not risk the anger of their fellows by speaking out.

Cowards, I thought, throwing another nicely duplicitous glance in Coxes For Brains' direction as I did so.

And yet it must all have looked very different from the pulpit, for the service moved serenely on, from mismatched song to confusing allegory, and on to the next lesson.

He's got a good voice for this, I realised, looking up at Norman in his element; and he isn't so awkward when he knows what he's talking about.

He wasn't awkward at all, actually. He flowed confidently through the service, speaking kindly but not patronisingly, finding interest in small things, yet again and again returning as if quite naturally to his main theme. He seemed so sure of his belief that people should and could just be *nice* to one another that he should have persuaded everyone by the sheer force of his will.

I wondered what made his certainty so different from that of the stone faced wolves lurking amongst his flock. Perhaps it was the sense that he had thought about these things, and was now simply sharing his conclusions. That somehow or other he had devoted himself to the study of human nature, and of a dense, confusing, and often self-contradictory book, and had come to the conclusion that people were basically good.

I looked up a his beaming, hopeful face, and determined that he should not be disappointed.

It was a form of charisma, I realised, quite different from the intense, hypnotic power affected by the idiot now dramatically refusing a drink beside me, but more genuine, and infinitely more moving.

It was just a shame it was wasted on this lot.

Someone passed me a biscuit and, still musing on the contradictory nature of mankind, I ate it.

Oh God.

Oh, mighty and fearsome God of the blood-soaked harvest corn: that was terrible.

A gifted speaker Norman might be, but a baker he was not.
The thing was thin and fragile, but so dry it seemed to steal all the moisture from my mouth. I tried to swallow, but only choked on the mouthful of flavourless crumbs, eliciting a chiding *"Hush"* from a complacent matron on the bench in front of me.

Eyes watering, I groped blindly past the dark eyed Prince of Granny Smiths and interrupted his latest soliloquy to seize the proffered chalice and wash the horror away.

It *wasn't "...wine"* anyway. It was porter, Tom's best: rich and sweet and full bodied, and if this was what it was like before it had properly settled, I couldn't imagine what it would be like next week. Always supposing there would *be* a next week.

I took another swig, to wash the taste out of my mouth, and then another, and I probably would have had a fourth if Molly hadn't elbowed me in the ribs and made me hand over the goblet.

It was mostly empty by then, anyway.

Soon after this the service seemed to wrap up, and as everyone clambered to their feet and began pulling theirselves together again, there came a sense from the general bustle that, while all that talk might have been a lot of old nonsense, you couldn't go wrong with a good sing-song and a cup of something.

It was a shame, really, opined the complacent woman, that we were going to burn the poor fellow, but then we couldn't have everything, could we?

I considered pointing out that we could always *not* burn him, and see what happened, but she had already turned away. So we joined the general bustle of hat-bearing people winding, far more decorously than they had got in, through the church and out into the daylight.

As Molly and I got closer to the door I noticed Reverend Poltwhistle had stationed himself outside and was attempting to exchange a few words with each person as they left the church.

It was a nice thought, but after two hours of listening to him talk, I could tell that most were more interested in getting out of there than they were in hearing anything more from that quarter.

I could see their point, really: even worried as I was, after all that porter what I mostly wanted was to get out of the crowd and find a privy. So we were moving at a fair rate when all at once our crocodile faltered and then stopped altogether.

"Ah, Reverend!" Of course: the Lord of the Apple Trees had to ruin it for everyone. Well, not everyone, I admitted, granting him justice if only in the privacy of my mind: most of the congregation had already escaped by this point, and were no doubt already skipping up the hill to the Inn like so many murderous woolly lambs. But he was ruining it for me, and that was what really mattered.

"A very fine sermon, Reverend," intoned the King in Russets; "I can see that you have much to...*offer*."

"Oh, do you think so?" he perked up a little; "Everyone rushed off so quickly, I wasn't at all sure they liked it, you know. I wondered if I had said something amiss, perhaps put someone's nose a little - ah - out of joint, so to speak. It can be so easy to make oneself unwelcome."

"I can assure you, dear sir, your presence is *very* welcome. Indeed, I am quite sure that you will prove a... *blessing* to us all."

I shifted uncomfortably from foot to foot: should I interrupt him, or should I not?

On the one hand, just listening to this overblown nonsense was making me shudder.

On the other, Himself was trying so very hard to be a sinister and Machiavellian figure, that it was possible even someone as cheerfully oblivious as Norman Poltwhistle would eventually realise something was going on.

On a secret, terrible and squamous third hand, hidden beyond the ken of mortal man, though... I *really* needed to find a privy.

I was saved from my deliberations by a couple of stone faced true believers who had been standing against a wall like a pair of particularly unimaginative gargoyles. They had clearly had similar thoughts to my own, and now moved in to intercept Himself before he could give the game away completely.

He was just explaining that "The island has long awaited such a... *sacrament*" with so much significant emphasis I was surprised his eyebrows didn't drop off, and I could see that any minute now he was going to start harping on about his blessed apple trees, when they pulled up in front of him, tugging their forelocks like the world's sternest and most unconvincing old retainers.

"Begging your pardon my lord," said the first, in tones neither of apology nor of deference.

"But you're needed," added the second.

"Urgently."

"Very urgently."

"On private business."

"Very private."

Himself drew breath to say something magnanimous and yet chilling, but they rolled straight over him."And *secret* my lord."

"Very secret."

"It's probably about the apple trees." I muttered, sarcastically. Which in other circumstances would have been a mistake.

Because he heard me.

"Ah, the apple trees, of course." He gave a small, secret smile, pausing for a moment to make sure everyone had noticed it.

"Lead on then my men. And, Reverend?" he turned a little, sweeping one arm around as though he was pulling an imaginary cloak dramatically about himself, "Until we… meet again."

And he swept away between the two blank-faced men, doing his best to look like a mysteriously menacing presence and not like a schoolboy being dragged away for a good scolding.

The Reverend shook himself slightly as they turned away, and I felt a little shudder of glee because *Norman didn't like him either.* Then he noticed that we were still waiting.

"Oh! Dora, Molly, how nice to see you here! And what did you think of the service?"

"It was lovely! Wasn't it Dor'?" Honestly! There was no need for Molly to jab me in the ribs like that.

"It was, really lovely" I agreed, more truthfully than I had expected. "Everyone really enjoyed the singing, and," I shifted awkwardly, less from bashfulness than from other, more pressing concerns; "and I think you spoke most awfully well, sir." I burst out figuratively, if not literally.

Molly, clearly mistaking my discomfort for some symptom of Romance, nodded encouragingly: "She was just telling me so, sir: "Lovely clear voice he's got," she said; didn't you, Dora?"

I smiled, gritting my teeth both at Molly's assistance and at my own discomfort, and nodded frantically. "Very eloquent," I managed.

He beamed at us both: "Oh now that is very kind of you, very kind indeed."

"I didn't understand it all," or at all; "but it sounded beautiful." Molly added encouragingly. "And of course a bit to drink never goes amiss."

"Ah, well," he gave an awkward, self deprecating sort of laugh "I can hardly be held responsible for *that* innovation, but I must say Tom's porter seems to have been very well received."

He glanced behind us, "He isn't with you?"

"No, um, he was but..." I tailed off, not sure how to explain.

"He didn't like the noise, sir." said Molly, frankly.

"Oh, of course, very sensible," smiled Norman, seeming somehow entirely unoffended by the idea of a person's needs jarring with his own sense of social convention."Well, we must be sure to let him know it was appreciated."

"Now," he smiled at us both, "I mustn't keep you: I know taverns are always overrun after a service."

What? But I thought we weren't supposed to work!

"I know," he grinned at my look of shock; "I'm meant to be terribly disapproving, I'm sure, but I can hardly blame people for wanting to socialise a little after church, now, can I?" It was a nice smile, too, damn him.

"So you'd better go and help Tom before your patrons start a riot, and I'll do my best to be blissfully unaware when I come in later."

I was so confused by this latest revelation I couldn't even appreciate the irony of this statement, but just gave a vague, hesitant nod and started off down the path.

As we approached the space where the gate should have been he called out "Oh, and Dora!"

I turned back. "I thought tomorrow morning for our walk, if you can manage it.

About eleven o'clock?

We can bring a picnic."

11

I all but flew up the hill.

Not because I suspected Norman Poltwhistle was right when he guessed that the Inn would be full to the gills by the time we got there.

Not even because I really, *really* needed to find a privy. In fact, that rather slowed me down, confirming my long-held belief that whoever had designed the human body must have been drunk as a newt when they did so.

It was because I had an idea.

Not just an idea in fact: it was a *plan*. And it needed only a very little work to become a brilliant plan.

Accordingly I left Molly staring in my wake and hared off up the hill like, well like a hare, probably. We only have rabbits on the Island, so it's a little hard to be sure.

Anyway, I ran up the hill like *something very fast indeed* and even with a quick diversion in the inn-yard, I still managed to beat her through the door.

Norman was right: the place was packed to the gills. Nearly everyone who had been in church that morning was crammed into a corner, discussing the event in frantic undertones. So were quite a few who hadn't, for that matter.

I noticed Netta Stanley was there again, leaning on the bar with an oddly wistful expression, and so seemingly unaware of the way the crush gave way to a bubble of solitude all around her that I grew surer than ever that she must be up to something. Old Man Morris was crammed into his corner by the fire, nodding sagely and beaming all over his wrinkled face. Even Himself seemed to have shaken off his minders and was holding forth about something or other in a sonorously sinister whisper.

So I could understand Molly's being a little put out when, having liberated Tom from behind the bar, I promptly walked straight out of the taproom and into the kitchen.

She came in and glared at me once there was a lull in the crowd, but the effect was somewhat spoilt by the fact that she had to cough at me about three times before I noticed her.

I looked up from my reading: "Sorry Moll: did you need something?"

"I'm glaring at you"

"Are you?" I considered this news.

Glaring, on Molly, was not a particularly fearsome sight. She tried, but no matter how intently she stared she still gave more the impression of a girl in a ballad, gazing tragically into the distance, maybe longing for her true love that's far far away, than of eyes alight with foreboding rage.

I did my best to look cowed, anyway. What else are friends for?

"I'm sorry, Moll, is it really heaving out there?" I bit my lip in genuine contrition.

Or as close as I could get when I remembered all the times she'd stuck *me* with a bar full of thirsty gannets with the patience of over-tired toddlers.

"I'd be out there with you, you know I would, only I'm running out of time, and I've just got to get this done"

She relaxed her glare to the level of a Lovely Nancy farewelling her sailor lover, while safe in the knowledge that another true love would be along with the next ship.

"What the heck are you doing down there anyway?"

I gave her question due consideration "Planning."

"Planning?"

I reconsidered: "*Maybe* plotting."

Nancy seemed suddenly to regret her earlier insouciance: wide eyes grazed the skyline where no doubt her beloved's ship had just dipped out of sight.

"*What* are you plotting?"

"A picnic."

The eyes became more wistful, the cruel sea threatened to sink the little ship below the salt cold waves, and I thought I'd better say something more before she ran her boat against the rocks and lost her temper with me entirely.

"A *romantic* picnic, Molly. For the Reverend and me. I've got to come up with something: there's only two days left!"

Her eyes eased their assault then abandoned folk music altogether.

I considered saying "I *love him*, Molly," an argument that had worked on me more often than was remotely reasonable, but somehow I couldn't quite do it.

It wasn't that I couldn't tell a lie: I'd been lying to all and sundry ever since I was old enough to say *No, Gammer, I can't think where those footprints came from.*

It wasn't even that I couldn't stand the thought of manipulating my oldest, dearest friend. Molly and I had been manipulating and taking advantage of one another ever since we both came to work at the Inn.

By this time it was more a game than anything else.

What made the words stick in my throat was the fact that it *wouldn't* be a lie, or not quite.

I didn't love him. Not the way Molly thought. Not even the way I loved her, and Tom and, alright, maybe that ruddy cockerel but don't tell him I said that.

But I was beginning to *like* him.

Somehow, in the face of that, the thought of persuading poor, sweet, open-hearted Molly that I was desperately in love... Well, it left a bad taste in my mouth.

"*Please*, Moll".

To my horror I felt my face growing hot, my vision began to wobble madly, and I realised my eyes were filling with tears. I wasn't desperately in love. What I was, was just desperate.

Molly softened all at once: "Sorry Dora, I wasn't thinking."

She gave me an oddly gentle kind of smile: the kind you give to worried mothers on stormy nights, or to a child who's found an injured butterfly. Or Molly herself, after a night with Jimmy The Bastard Bettan. It felt strange seeing it on someone else's face, instead of feeling it on my own.

"The bar's not so bad now they've all got a mug, I can get by for the rest of the night." She patted me on the shoulder in a vaguely comforting way, as if I were a strange horse that had got into the yard and was liable to panic at unexpected noises.

"You just stay here and plan your picnic, and it'll all come out right as rain, you wait and see."

I wanted to make some joke about not having it rain on my picnic, or not having *time* to wait, but somehow the two got muddled up and all I managed was a little choked gasp.

Molly patted me some more, in an optimistic sort of way, then darted out of the kitchen again. As the door eased shut I heard her sweet voice calling "You put that down and get out from behind there or else I'll lamp you one with the tapping mallet," but there was no sound of retaliation, so I supposed things must be quieting down out there after all.

I returned to my books.

The thing was, I couldn't just throw together any old picnic. Picnics weren't exactly common on the Island, everyone being either too hard at work or too inadequately provisioned, or both, but even by the standards of the picnics we didn't have, this needed to be something special. Hence my sudden enthusiasm for research. In theory the cookery books lived in the kitchen so they would be handy for everyday use.

It had seemed logical enough when I put them there: cookery books - cook - kitchen, but in practice, after the first few experimental flourishes, Molly and I just made the same four or five dishes every time and never needed to look at a book for any of them.

We were creatures of habit, for the most part, and while we might sometimes pore over the cramped pages and wonder what the mysteriously described delights might taste like in theory, in practice we had neither the time nor the patience to find out. We learned that lesson with the Everlasting Syllabub.

Besides, persuade Tom to try any form of curry I could not and would not attempt. At least you knew what you were getting with a stargazey pie.

So my mother's store of recipes and household management sat in solemn splendour on the pantry shelf where, apart from our occasional flights of fancy and the odd stubborn collar-stain, they were seldom ever disturbed.

Today though I had them all down, spread out around me on the cool stone flags, their yellowed pages ruffled at the edges like, I imagined, so many lilies on a pond.

I went from book to book like a particularly fussy frog, never settling long wherever I landed, but scrabbling frantically through the tightly packed text in a way that completely ruined my analogy.

I knew I had seen it somewhere. I remembered turning the water stained pages, scrolling my finger down blurring lines of text, looking for *something* then encountering instead, the completely unexpected and inexplicable heading: *Aphrodisiacs*.

I recalled perfectly my initial confusion, the dawning light of understanding giving way to hilarity, Molly's giggles as I dragged her over to see what I had found.

There had been illustrations, I remembered, ones that I hadn't understood, and that Molly had understood so well that she had had to sit down for a while to get her breath back, and Tom had come in from the yard to make sure no one was badly hurt.

I suspected the illustrations would make more sense now, although I doubted I'd find them as funny as Molly had.

I remembered our whispered conversation, later that night: *Would you ever... How could anybody... Do you think they really work?!* Molly had declared her instant willingness to try any and all of the recipes therein just as soon as any kind of a true love should arrive to be experimented on, while I, I recalled with bitter irony, had been equally emphatic in insisting that I would not.

All this I remembered perfectly. What I didn't remember, not even in the smallest of insignificant details, was what any of it had actually said.

Somehow, possibly even because of how frantically I was looking, rather than despite it, I managed to go through every book a good four times before I found what I wanted.

It wasn't - perfect memory be damned - in one book at all, but in three: the aforementioned chapter proving more of a letter of reproach than anything of practical use, the recipes hiding coyly under the heading of "household remedies" and the illustrations inexplicably sandwiched between a page of advice on the deportment of young ladies on the occasion of their come out, and a recipe for wedding cake. Still, I found what I needed eventually.

Or rather I didn't.

It dawned on me, peering at the crabbed, water spotted pages, that there was another reason I didn't use these recipes much. They all called for things that, like hares and apples, and lily ponds for that matter, the Island simply didn't have.

I squinted uncertainly at a reference to "sparrowgrass", wondering exactly what that was. It didn't, going by the no less unfunny illustrations, look like anything that grew around here.

I was sure I'd have heard about it if it did.

People would have made *observations* about it.

I wondered whether goosegrass would do instead. Probably not, if those pictures were to be believed.

Oysters were easier: I knew what oysters were. Knowing wouldn't help me get my hands on any, it was true, but at least I knew what I wasn't getting my hands on. The Island had plenty of shellfish: I could improvise.

But a lot of the suggested foods were completely inexplicable: pine nuts would be nuts from a pine tree, obviously, but what in the ever burning realm of the ever ravenous God was a mirliton?

As for "love apples", well, I decided there were some things I simply didn't want to know.

Still, once I had eliminated all the impossibilities there remained a handful of recipes that were, at worst, only mildly improbable.

I set to work with a will and, even with some time lost to burning a chicken hash and a dish of turnips for the Reverend's dinner, soon achieved a fairly creditable dish of honeyed fritters.

I set these under the window to cool, and turned to the next feasible-looking page of the book.

This called itself a soffritto, but by the look of things that was just a fancy way of saying "minced beef".

I scowled at the recipe: beef wasn't impossible to come by, by any means, but it wasn't cheap either, particularly at this time of year. I was starting to wonder if the book was doing this on purpose.

I shook off my suspicions and got to work. I *had* some beef, at least: a good sized piece of it too, and decently aged, that I'd been keeping for Tom's birthday next week. Still, needs must when bloodthirsty islanders plot to sacrifice innocent vicars: I took up my knife and began chopping.

Tom would just have to be content with fish on his birthday.

I ignored the suspicion that Tom would, in fact, *prefer* the familiarity of fish to the excitement of roast beef, and for the very reason that it was familiar.

It was about the intention of the thing.

I would just have to find him some other incredibly thoughtful, considerate token of my friendship, once the present excitement was finished with. It couldn't be that much harder than saving an idiot's life and getting away with it under the eye of the whole murderous community.

I chopped faster.

Mind you, I mused as I patted browned, seasoned meat into shape upon a platter, expense seemed to be something of a theme with these recipes.

It seemed there were three basic routes one could take when trying to get to point B (a man's heart) by way of point A (his stomach).

There was the excessive -and often revolting- option: eggs coddled in ambergris, rare fruits, exquisite wines, other, less appetising-sounding eggs dug out of the innards of particularly hard-to-find fish, and various mysterious lumps that sounded far more trouble than they were worth.

Then there was the medicinal: leaves with fragrances supposed to titillate the senses, fruits said to stimulate the blood, spices to heat the appetite. All of which, as well as sounding frankly more than a little unbelievable, was, again, quite staggeringly expensive.

Last of all there were the...

There were...

Well, there were the *analogies*.

These were the dishes designed to make Molly snigger.

Suggestive peaches, improbable parsnips, desserts that towered over the dinner table without even a scrap of euphemism on. All of them designed to lightly turn the mind to thoughts of love.

The confection politely translated as "cream horns" had looked surprisingly plausible: at the least I had a light hand for pastry, and we had some cream set by for porridge and the like. Still I rejected it out of hand: why any man would want to watch someone take a healthy bite out of *that* was beyond me.

I sighed and cracked a couple of eggs to apply the finishing touch to my creation.

I looked down, basking in the warmth and satisfaction of a difficult job well done.

I blinked and looked again.

I squeezed my eyes shut in the vain hope that when I opened them the entire mess would have mysteriously disappeared.

I pried one eye open again and risked a glimpse. It hadn't

Two smooth, voluptuous, tawny mounds stared back at me, glossy with translucent egg-white, the amber yolks jiggling softly at their peaks.

It was, to say the least, analogous.

As I stared, dumbfounded, at the fruits of my labours, the kitchen door banged open. I started at the disturbance and, in my panic plunged both hands intemperately into the dish.

Molly sauntered into the room and looked at me oddly: "You alright there, Dor'?"

"Fine!" I gasped, nonchalantly, up past my elbows in half-cooked meat, "Never better, Molly."

"Do you need a hand with something?"

"No, thanks", I beamed desperately, "Everything's under control!"

I resisted the urge to wave a carefree, meat-smeared hand. She continued to stare.

"Did you want something, Moll?" I enquired through my gritted grin.

"Just getting the Reverend his dinner."

She ambled across to the oven and pried out the golden brown dishes, then leaned against the wall to look at me.

She wore the conflicted grin of one who sees a friend insist that she is not having the problem she is very clearly having, and who wants to help but, at the same time, wants desperately to find out just how far she can push it.

"Want me to save you some?" she suggested, idly scraping meat and vegetables onto the plates.

"No, thank you", I replied as politely as one could while marinating up to the armpits in bust tartare.

"You sure?"

"Quite sure."

"And you're certain you don't want any help?"

I smiled tightly.

"Well, if you say so," and with a last glance at my meat-immured arms, she wandered out again, smirking horribly, the plates balanced attractively at her hip.

I glowered down at the dish in front of me.

There was no hope of returning it to its terrifying glories now.

Abandoning the attempt with no little sense of relief, I patted the mess of meat and eggs into a rough rectangle, seasoned it aggressively, and shoved it into the vacated oven. It would keep better that way anyway, I reasoned, scouring my hands under the pump, and I could slice it up nicely to fit a basket.

I tried not to think too hard about that.

12

The morning of the picnic dawned bright and inviting.

So much so that I was immediately suspicious.

I glared sceptically around the sunlit chamber, taking in the clean sparkle of glass in the window, the way the light kissed Molly's bounteous tresses, the fresh, springlike colours on the painted chamberpot. Yes: something, I decided, was definitely up.

I slid an apprehensive toe out of my blankets and lowered it gingerly to the floor.

The toe was back under the covers before I had time to blink. It was freezing out there.

Any sense of validation I might have felt at having my fears so readily confirmed was killed by the knowledge that I was going to have to get out of bed anyway.

I contemplated just wrapping my bedding around myself in a bundle and going about the rest of the day like that, but regretfully abandoned the idea.

Even if one could get through most of the running of an inn while dressed as a sort of human snail, I could find no rational excuse for going on a romantic picnic wearing approximately half a bed. Besides, while it would certainly provide a more comfortable conclusion to the event, I had never yet heard of anyone accomplishing a successful seduction while wearing a sheet, three woollen blankets, and a patchwork quilt.

I got up, shivered through washing and dressing, and set about the morning routine as briskly as possible, in the hope that this would warm me up a little.

It didn't, but I did learn that, against all the laws of natural philosophy, no matter where I went it was always colder than wherever I had been before. Step outside: the wind was bitter ice. Scurry back indoors: I was out of the sun, shivering on the cold, shadowed flagstones of the dark and chilly Inn. Go and feed the chickens: the poultry yard was drafty *and* shadowy *and* still damp from the rain, and the bloody cockerel had got himself stuck on a ledge and pecked me when I tried to help him down. And then he flapped down by himself. Leave the poultry yard and, well, you get the idea.

Still, while the taproom fire refused to warm anything beyond a small, scorching-hot area directly in front of it, by the time I had got the porridge ready and had borne Tom's bowl out to the suddenly inviting fug of the brewing shed, the biting cold had begun to lose its edge a little, and a tour of the Island's hills and shore began to seem a little less like a torture designed for the express purpose of tormenting over-educated barmaids who tried to interfere with the smooth running of the Island's macabre devotions and more like a healthy, wholesome activity that might, if I managed things correctly, be brought to a satisfyingly unwholesome conclusion.

I was further strengthened in my resolve by the appearance of Molly who, apparently now fully recovered from the indignity of having to manage the bar all by herself for the second time this week, not only attempted to coax my rebellious curls into something more suited to a seduction over the nuncheon nibbles, but produced from somewhere a thick blanket and a small basket of wild strawberries.

I accepted Molly's assurances that the blanket was sturdy and comfortable, and would keep away both mud and intrusive prickly things, and tried not to wonder just how thoroughly she had tested this, or how well it had been laundered afterwards. As a committed shirker of the wash, I was afraid I wouldn't much like the answer.

As for the strawberries, they were small, and bright red, and I had no idea how or where she had found them at this time of year, but I strongly suspected a midden was involved. I didn't care: my books had spoken very warmly of the enticing allure of the strawberry, and they would round out the picnic nicely. Besides, the Poet had once told me that the strawberry was the only fruit that tasted sweeter than it really was, which made no sense at all but was about as allegorical as I was prepared to get.

I hugged Molly fondly, and she had just time for a whispered "Good luck, Dor'" before Norman Poltwhistle descended the stairs, beaming in anticipation and with his greatcoat folded over one arm.

I considered the greatcoat dubiously.

On the one hand, it made him look like a demented crow and would prove a definite hindrance to the soaking and subsequent removal of his clothes, should it come on to rain - which was, I acknowledged, by and large the point of a coat, unhelpful as I might find it.

On the other hand, it was a very large and billowing sort of a greatcoat so if it did rain, perhaps he might be persuaded to wrap it around me, quelling my artistic shivers with his warmth, pressing my lissom form against his manly chest and...Well, and so on.

I shook my head and ladled out the porridge: even in fantasies that painted me as nubile and pliant I could not convince myself to imagine Norman Poltwhistle's physique into any adjectives other than "bony" and "very probably pigeon".

I dipped some honey into his porridge, and added an extra spoonful to mine. The books had been even keener on honey than they were on strawberries, and frankly, we needed all the help we could get.

Breakfast done and the plates squirrelled away into the scullery where Molly, if she wouldn't actually wash them, at least wouldn't have to keep looking at them, I hoisted my basket and my blanket and we set out on our way.

There was some small debate about our best course for the day.

Norman had thought to walk along the coastline, heading inland whenever the shoreline became impassable, or when some interesting landmark presented itself.

I disputed this, firstly on the grounds that all the most interesting landmarks were in the hills; secondly that while other beaches might have the decency to be composed of smooth, golden sands, ours was largely made up of a constantly damp, gritty shingle that slithered under foot, trapped feet, got inside the strongest, best laced of boots, and made walking anywhere an unremitting, tortuous slog; and finally, when all else failed, that ours was, after all, a working island, and while the little boats and the tall, brooding forms of the fishing sheds might seem very picturesque at a distance, the reality meant beaches littered with crab claws, the scent of rotting fishguts, and a labyrinth of snaring scraps of net, slurried quicksand, and tar that wouldn't come out of your clothes for love nor money.

Also, and I could not emphasise this firmly enough, seagulls.

Big, bad tempered, vicious ones with beaks that could peck through stone. Well, sandstone, anyway.

In the face of these arguments Norman folded entirely, but he seemed so dejected at my comprehensive dismissal of all his plans that I relented slightly, allowing that there were several pretty, sandy coves that we might perhaps be able to visit in the course of the day, always supposing that the tide wasn't in at the time.

"And you know, Sir, that the view from our hilltop will be wonderful," I added, consolingly; "why, on a day like this you should be able to see all the way across the water back to your own home." Talk of home seemed to lower his spirits still more, but he did his best to rally a little as we turned onto the path out of the inn yard and up the hill, away from the church and the squat, brown houses that led to the coast road below.

"These coves," he persisted, puffing slightly as we approached the brink of the hill; "I suppose they're terribly, um, secluded and -ah- romantic?"

This was more like it!

"Very romantic" I assented cheerfully.

If you like wet feet and sand in your drawers I firmly did not add.

"And secluded?"

"Well, most of them are in view of the fishing boats," I admitted; "but there's a couple that are hidden behind the rocks," I added, hastily; "And once the fleet's come in they're all quiet as anything: no one would ever bother us - bother you I mean - at all, Sir."

"And I would imagine," he mused; "that they're quite beautiful after dark, with the moonlight on the water and so on."

I made a noise that could be mistaken for assent, and kept walking.

On reflection, I suggested we bring our hike to its conclusion at some western cove or other around sunset, when the light on the water really would be very attractive, and things would be as secluded as I could manage, between one fleet coming in and another going out.

Resolution gave me a burst of speed and I pushed on up the hill, flinging my arms wide at its crest. "And there's your view, Sir!" I declared, victorious; "isn't it lovely?"

He stopped for a moment, not saying a word, and I turned to him, half-wondering if the hill had been too much for him, and perhaps we should go back and take the coast road round anyway.

But he was gazing out, over the Island and the glittering water to the mainland with a miniature village, barely recognisable in the distance. "Yes," he murmured, so quietly I could barely hear it; "Quite lovely."

On the whole, our exploration was not quite the aid to flirtation I had hoped.

The Island isn't big, by any means, but it is hilly: as though someone had taken a much larger, flatter place and crumpled it up like a sheet of paper.

There's a nice, straightforward road running through the middle of course, and a handful of smaller paths that are usually enough to get most people wherever they need to be, so generally speaking this isn't a problem. Everything that isn't on the main road, though, is either uphill or down or occasionally both.

The problem with fascinating historical landmarks far from the beaten path, of course, is...well the clue's in the name, really isn't it?

And the problem with both preaching and barmaiding as professions is that while they might provide plenty of opportunities to develop one's muscles by means of thumping bibles, hefting casks and so on, they leave one with very little time to accustom oneself to taking long, healthy walks in the countryside.

His legs were longer than mine, too, which meant keeping pace with one another was difficult, and walking arm in arm, if I had dared suggest such a thing, nigh on impossible.

Add this to the steep slopes of the hills, which left me too out of breath to attempt much by way of charming repartee even if I thought he would be able to hear it over his huffing and wheezing -and perhaps we really should have taken the coast road after all- and my plans seemed doomed before we had even begun.

But eventually we fell into a pattern of sorts, flinging ourselves up the hills with as much vigour as a rather spindly vicar and a... *voluptuous* barmaid could command, catching our breath and sharing a few observations -yes, it was *very* bright today wasn't it? And yes, you could see the mainland from *this* hilltop *too*, before hobbling down as best we could on the other side.

In between hills we ambled, not arm in arm perhaps, but companionably enough: he discovering fascinating wildflowers and herbs upon the rocky sward, and I answering his questions on Island history, and trying to keep him out of the stinging nettles.

It was as I responded to some minor enquiry or other that I realised the greatest problem with my plan.

In attempting to take Norman on a romantic tour of the Island I had neglected to consider one very important point: the Island was not romantic *at all*.

The mistake, I felt, was understandable. My original idea had been to confront Norman with all the ghastliest bits of stone I could uncover, in the hope of scaring him off with a parade of horrors, and thus *avoid* the more traditional means of rendering him unfit for purpose. It had been a good plan, and I had had every faith that it would work. That I should, in the shock of finding the Reverend in possession of a backbone, forget this aspect of our projected picnic was quite forgivable: I had, after all, had other things on my mind.

Like the fact that he, apparently, hadn't.

Now however I was confronted with a problem. How could I turn our ubiquitously gruesome past into the stuff of romantic dalliance?

The answer was: I couldn't.

While the views from our umpteen hilltops were uniformly breathtaking, and the sea did indeed look thoroughly charming at sunset -I could not speak for the sunrise, having a firm policy of not being awake in time to find out- the truth was that our life was one of mud, more mud and misery, occasionally punctuated by moments of astonishing violence; and the local landmarks reflected this fact.

Perhaps in the right light the brooding, shadowy forms of the fishing sheds might look merely quaint, but even in a deep fog there was no way I could pass off, say, the ancient cairn of broken skulls where those who trespassed in the sacred groves used to have their brains dashed out with a pointy rock as some kind of whimsical folk art.

Well I *could*, probably, if I put my mind to it, but it would take a woman of vast ingenuity, creativity and fortitude to invent a believably innocent provenance for every revolting monument on our revolting rock.

Assuming that I was not that woman, I was going to have to settle for the truth.

I paused for a moment, struck by the sudden realisation that I had not spoken the honest truth even once, to anyone, since Norman Poltwhistle first walked into the Inn.

I mean, I must have done. There must have been some moment when I had made some straightforward comment, about beer, perhaps, or the weather, or some point in Aristotle's *Dialogue on Nicomachean Ethics*, but try as I might, I couldn't bring one to mind.

"Are you alright there, Dora?" the Reverend huffed to a stop and waited for me to catch up.

"Oh, fine, Sir: I was just catching my breath" I answered automatically.

See? There you go again!

Right then, I decided, The Truth: how hard could it be?

In fact, I mused, there could even be some advantages to telling the truth, always supposing Norman wasn't scared completely witless.

He must be reasonably interested in history, or he would never have suggested this excursion in the first place. Perhaps I could fascinate him with some small details of local lore or, if that didn't work, perhaps I could introduce him to local lore and then pretend to *be* fascinated while he explained it all to me.

I could shudder artistically at the gory bits and he could lay a steadying hand upon my tender arm and...well, it was worth a try. And there was always the faint chance that it would scare him silly after all.

Right. I henceforth swore to speak nothing but the whole, honest, unadorned truth for the rest of the day.

Except about the sacrifice thing, obviously.

And not if it would hurt someone's feelings.

And I simply *couldn't* let Molly know my long-awaited romance was a sham.

She would be so *sad*.

But apart from that I would be a veritable beacon of truthfulness.

It couldn't be that hard, surely.

I took him to the skull-pile first, because it was nearest.

"Fascinating!" he remarked, peering into a late lamented lug-hole; "and you say no one knows why they're here?"

"No, Sir." *Ease into the truth, ease into it.*

"My word!" he peered closer, "could it have something to do with druids, do you think?"

Out of all the myriad strange, arcane, and downright obtuse customs he might have associated with the Island, he had somehow managed to land on the one thing we didn't have. "I've never heard of druids round here."

See? You're doing better already!

He looked disappointed: "Really? Well perhaps if one were to dig *under* the mound, one might find some sign of..."

"Oh, they did that Sir."

"They did?"

"When I was about twelve", I was on firmer ground here; "Mercy Wainright and Billy Cooper dug all around these parts, looking for buried treasure."

"And did they find anything" his eyes gleamed with suppressed hope. Fortunately, I was able to reward him.

"They did Sir, right under this very mound, and a horrible mess they made of it too. Missus Wainright was furious when she saw what Mercy'd done to her good boots, and Mister Cooper made them put all the skulls back, and wouldn't let Billy set foot in their house till he swore by...he swore it was all exactly as he found it."

"But what did they find?"

"They found another skull, Sir."

I couldn't help thinking he looked a little disappointed somehow.

I tried again: "I mean, they found another skull, *Norman*."

It didn't help.

"Just another skull?"

"Yes, Sir, Norman I mean, but this one was strange and twisted, with great, gnarled horns and a single terrible eye."

There. Both true and grotesque. I was getting the hang of this.

He looked fascinated: "And what became of the skull? Did they re-bury it? Do they perhaps have it still? I must say, I should be very interested to see it."

Mercy stuck it on a pole and tried to bring it back to life in a diabolical ritual mostly cribbed from The Ballad Of James Harris, and when that didn't work she smashed it with the poker and sulked for a week.

"Nobody knows"

And I was doing so well!

Oh well, in for a penny and so on: "It simply disappeared"

This cheered him up immensely, so I filed my falsehood under "if it would hurt someone's feelings" and basked in the warm glow of a spotless conscience.

"But how mysterious!"

"Yes, isn't it?" the *skull* was mysterious, not the disappearance, just the skull; "Shall we carry on? There are some wonderful ruins over the next hill".

And so we did.

13

After that everything seemed to fall into place.

We'd walk in companionable short-windedness to some unspeakable landmark, I'd explain what we were looking at, he'd ask a few excited questions, and I'd answer to the best of my ability as we puffed our way to the next horrid rockery or what-have-you.

Of course there were a few awkward moments, like the time I pointed out the Actor's house in the distance and told Norman how he'd lurked there, on the path over the hill, waiting for some unwary traveller to come by, when he'd leap forth, dash out their brains with the hilt of an old sword and drag them back to his house.

"... and then he'd eat them," I concluded; "but eventually so many people went missing that a party was sent out to see what had happened to everyone, and he tried to fight them all at once, except his sword was only a stage prop, so he was overpowered almost immediately and everything brought to light.

They say the house was a terrible sight when they looked inside: arms and legs hanging from the beams, and preserving jars full of brains and kidneys and things, and someone's heart stewing over the fire."

I paused for effect and also because if I hadn't then the next thing out of my mouth would have been "But I think they made that part up, because everyone knows that heart is better fried" which would have somewhat ruined the effect.

Well that part had gone very well: Norman said "Really?" and "Goodness me" and "Oh, dear God no!" at all the appropriate moments, and I'd just started explaining how the Actor had been flung to his death from the cliff top, and how he'd been ranting the whole way down, and how they said he'd been driven mad because every character he ever played had died before the third act, death scene after death scene, so he'd come out here where no one would know him, meaning to make other people perform the death scenes for him for a change, and alright maybe that last part's all conjecture but it makes sense, don't you think, when all of a sudden Norman burst out laughing.

I was just trying to come to terms with this strange lack of sensibility when he flashed an unexpectedly boyish smile and said: "You see, this is why I love history: the stories are so wonderfully ghoulish and nobody ever blinks an eye at ones being interested in them. Now if something of that sort were to occur in the present day it would be quite a different matter." After which I somehow couldn't bring myself to say "But this was last January" and I didn't want to lie and ruin a two hour streak of total honesty, so I wound up saying nothing and we strolled along to the next ruddy artefact with him beaming all the while and chattering cheerfully about how much *fun* my murderous, bloody heritage apparently was.

Not wanting to get soaked to the skin before we'd at least had some lunch, I skipped the waterfall where the Poet used to stand being dramatically melancholy and getting his boots wet, and took us straight to the unholy well instead.

That proved to be a mistake.

"But you must mean a holy well" Norman argued.

"Unholy" I retorted firmly.

"But if a man was killed for teaching the word of God, that's clearly martyrdom. The well probably sprang up where his blood touched the earth or something."

He looked awfully keen on this idea, so I didn't bother to explain that the well had *been* holy until his putative Saint had come stamping around in his medieval size nines, upsetting everybody and fouling up the well water with his sacrilegious corpse, but just set my lip and scowled mutinously. "Unholy."

"But it's such a classic example: a pious man, struck down for his adherence to the true faith, and from his sainted wounds there arises a font of pure, baptismal water to bless..."

"Look, who's leading this tour anyway, me or you?"

"You, of course, but..."

I glared at him "Un. Holy."

"But why?"

"Because," I declared; "he lost."

At this retort Norman's mouth fell open.

He closed it again, and opened it, and drew breath to say something, but exactly what it was going to be I'll never know, because at that point everything seemed so tense and argumentative that I panicked and splashed him with the water from the definitely desanctified well.

This, inexplicably, seemed to have been the right thing to do, for he splashed me back, and laughed, and we set off again in high good humour with him trying to think of a name for his supposed saint, and telling stories about people who'd swum through whirlpools, survived beheadings, or held conversations with the local shrubberies. He was just rounding off The Life Of Saint Christina The Frankly Bonkers, when the next landmark hove into view and we came to a sudden, uncomfortable stop.

The great Sentinel Stone stood, tall, black and implacable, like a gateway to some different, bleaker realm.

Which sounds terribly mysterious and intriguing when you read it, I'm sure, but life on the Island was quite bleak enough as it was, thank you very much.

Even Norman, who'd cheerfully prodded and poked at all the most disturbing scraps of history I'd found for him so far, fell abruptly silent in the shadow of the ancient stone.

The air felt still here, as though even the wind didn't like to come too near, and all the thousand tiny sounds of birds and insects that had gone unnoticed throughout our noisy clamberings became suddenly all too obvious in their absence.

I shifted uncomfortably, not wanting to look like an idiot who was afraid of a rock, and glanced at Norman quickly, out of the corner of my eye, to see how he was taking it.

Oh, good. He was standing there like an idiot too.

Somehow, knowing that I wasn't the only one to be unnerved by the looming monolith gave me courage.

"You know," I remarked as conversationally as I could; "I've lived here all my life and that thing still gives me the collywobbles."

"I don't blame you," he managed, somewhat breathlessly; "it's very... impressive, isn't it?"

"Bloody unnerving is what it is" I muttered under my breath, apparently less quietly than I had intended, for this startled a laugh out of him, and just like that the atmosphere broke.

I don't mean to say that the sun broke through the chilling gloom and the birds began once more to sing or anything like that, but all at once the creepiness seemed less overwhelming somehow, and we found ourselves grinning weakly at one another over our mutual foolishness. "Come on," I added, a little more confidently; "the wretched stone won't be able to see us once we're round this bend." and skirting carefully around the rock, just in case it should suddenly decide to abandon millennia of verticality and squash us flat, we made our way down past the Sentinel and into the glade beyond.

We weren't the only people to find the Sentinel Stone unnerving.

Looking at things sensibly there was no reason that this should be the case: it was no taller or gloomier than a fishing shed after all, and no lonelier than any of the other landmarks that littered our Island like toffee papers. Certainly it was less grisly than most. But something about its silent stillness made even the hardiest, heartiest soul think twice about coming too near.

Travellers gave it a wide berth; shepherds steered their flocks - never very keen on the place themselves - to further, less troubling fields; children dared one another to step into its shadow, then waited, dancing with nerves, for their turn to dart out, terrified and exhilarated, and brandish a toe into the darkened space beneath the unmoving stone.

Of course no one ever admitted it: the travellers and shepherds simply "felt like going the other way today," and the children, fear duly faced, would insist that they were never frightened at all, the momentary dash turning, in the retelling, into a hero's confident swagger, the dab of a toe into standing full in the shade "For at least an hour. Hours and hours probably, and I wasn't scared at all." But somehow, despite or perhaps because of such tales, the travellers never did feel like taking the path by the stone; the shepherds always seemed to know a different, better grazing, and as for the children: "We've done that, ages ago, I want to do something new." and off they'd go, to worry a neighbour's cows, or re-enact the tradition of sky-burial, or whatever else it was that children did.

All of which is to say that I didn't actually have any idea of what we were going to find.

"Stones," was all Old Man Morris would say, the one time I took it into my head to ask him. Then, after another mug or two of ale; "Carved stones." and not another word would he utter, but stared into the shadows, his eyes all a-glitter, as if dwelling on some secret memory.

So I suspected he'd never seen them either, Oldest Inhabitant or not.

Which is why I was quite as surprised as Norman was, when we rounded the corner and found, well, stones.

Carved stones.

They weren't in the least bit frightening.

That was the first thing I noticed, once the surprise of seeing them had worn off. They weren't tall and menacing, or disturbing and squat, and the carvings weren't particularly gruesome, even by mainland standards, they were just...odd.

They formed a rough sort of semi-circle, with a final, larger stone, either laid flat or fallen down in the centre. Their lower halves were completely obscured by the tall grass and wildflowers that, unchecked by sheep or scythe, ran riot here, but wherever they poked up I could see the tops of carved figures: very old and very strange indeed.

One had turned himself into a hoop, head to heels; another seemed to be becoming a tree -or coming out of one; a woman -very definitely a woman- brandished a coiling snake in each hand; while beside her, in worn relief, a young boy seemed quite unreasonably happy about being devoured by a bear.

I walked slowly round, as though in a daze, parting the long grasses to reveal figure after inexplicable figure, strange and obscure and -oh!

There was the Island God, looking not murderous or terrible at all, but just another strange carving of a skeletal man with great, barbed antlers, and long, boney claws; one figure among many.

I stepped back, dazed, one hand drifting to my brow as though to stop my reeling mind. *What could it mean?*

"What do you think they mean?"

This answer to my internal question almost stopped my heart.

Could it be that the stones themselves were speaking to me, telling me that the answer lay somewhere deep inside, in the ancient depths of my ancestral soul, curled and waiting for me to awaken it?

"I mean, they're awfully peculiar, aren't they?"

Or it could be Norman Poltwhistle.

I'd forgotten Norman. Somehow, in the dreamlike thrill of discovery, I had managed to forget all about the man I was supposed to be introducing to this place. The man whose life I supposed to be trying to save.

I eyed the stone with the God carved on distrustfully, and it gazed calmly back, as unmenacing as ever.

"Honestly," I answered, "I have no idea."

Now I suspect that if *I* were to visit some ancient ruin or mysterious artefact I would, assuming I had had the sense to enlist some local friend to come and explain everything, be somewhat put out to then discover that my companion had no more idea what we were looking at than I did. Norman, for some reason, was not.

Instead he seemed to view the whole thing as the most thrilling adventure imaginable.

"But it could be anything!" he declared, excitedly, "A monument, or a temple or..." he trailed off, clearly unable to think of any examples other than "monument" or "temple"; "...or *anything!*" he ended, rapturously.

"Not, *anything*, surely," I disagreed, unable to resist an argument even when my whole world has been quietly tipped askew; "I mean, it's hardly likely to have been a sheep shed, or a barbers shop, is it? It's much more likely it was just-" I groped for inspiration; "well, a temple perhaps, or... or a monument," I finished, lamely.

The words "ritual use" flitted inexplicably through my mind. "Or a graveyard!" I added, in sudden triumph.

"Oh do you think?" he looked intrigued: "I'd assumed the whole structure was built at once, with it being such a regular shape, but of course it's possible," he eyed one of the stones, wistfully, "I suppose one wouldn't quite like to dig and find out."

I had the distinct sense that if I had uttered anything even remotely resembling encouragement, he would have been pulling up the sod with his bare hands before I had time to breathe.

This would have been a bad idea at the best of times. Today, with the strangely unassuming figure of the God gazing blankly at us, reminding me that I had less than a day to go before the eager amateur excavator became so many charred leftovers, it struck me as a truly terrible one.

By way of a distraction I got out the lunch.

Food proved reasonably distracting. The minced beef... *thing* had held up pretty well, I felt, although I might try adding a few breadcrumbs next time, by way of holding it all together, and while I hadn't been able to find any oysters, Norman seemed uncommonly fond of winkles, polishing off most of the bag by himself before I'd even found myself a pin.

It was all very pleasant. So pleasant, in fact that most of the food was gone and I was leaning comfortably against one of the stones trying to eat a strawberry -*not* midden flavoured, thank you Molly- when I was struck by a terrible thought.

"Is it possible, do you think," I asked as casually as I could manage; "to profane a place with a fritter?"

Norman looked at me in mild confusion. Well of course he did: he had no idea what I was thinking about, and even if he could somehow look inside my head and see the wretched pile of skulls I'd shown him just that morning, he still wouldn't have made the connection.

Because I hadn't told him the bit about the sacred grove.

You know, the bit about the ancient priests doing horrible things with the heads of anyone who offended against it.

I looked around us: the lush grasses hummed with the industry of insects; two butterflies danced their silent battle in the sunlight; perched on one of the stones, a thrush piped. All was calm, idyllic... *grove*-y.

"Just as, um, a hyper-theatrical question" I added.

Yes, I know the word is hypothetical, but what I actually knew collided with what I thought he'd expect me to know, and in the heat of the moment I panicked. Look, it's hard work being an innocent, unspoiled country maid. Especially around these parts.

"Oh hypothetically?"

Bless the man for not over-emphasising the pronunciation.

"Yes, just," I waved vaguely about us; "say this place *was* a temple or a monument or something of that sort," he nodded encouragingly; "would it be a terrible offence do you think, to sit eating nuts and things, leaning on the carving of..." I checked the stone behind me; "of a girl with two, um, sort of fish... tail... things" I ended lamely.

"Oh, I shouldn't think so" he responded cheerfully.

"You don't?" I tried to keep the doubt out of my voice but, well, it was an awfully *big* pile of skulls.

"Not at all. The choir boys are forever eating nuts in church back home, and I've yet to threaten anyone with excommunication." He grinned: "Even if they *will* keep leaving the shells all over the choir stalls."

"No," he shook his head at my fancy; "I can't imagine any ancient priest taking offence at your basket of delicacies, my dear."

"Well," he gave an impish grin; "Not unless we refused to share the strawberries, at least."

I was not convinced: not least because, besides it's being really a very big pile of skulls indeed, I couldn't imagine the Reverend Norman Poltwhistle even at his most wrathful, threatening anyone with anything much more than some mild tutting, and perhaps a quiet sigh.

"Besides," he added cheerfully, "They're all dead now, so who could we possibly offend?"

Who indeed asked the silent figure of the God, with his mild unblinking eyes.

I ignored him: it wasn't as if they could smash someone's head in *and* burn them, after all.

Or they could, I supposed, but only one would count.

Right. Move along, Dora, you've no time to think about that now.

Don't think about dead priests, or angry deities, or really seriously creepy bits of rock. Don't ask yourself about the plots that may be unfolding, even now, without your knowledge. Forget about the fact that, actually, you weren't in any sort of danger at all until you decided to come to the rescue. Think of something else. Something pleasant.

He called you "my dear" a minute ago, didn't he? Forget the blasphemous biscuits and see what you can do with that.

I finished the strawberry in one bite and considered my surroundings with the Poet's eye: if ever there was an opportunity for reclining languidly upon a couch of flowers this was it.

I flung myself seductively to the ground.

Well, I tried to. In practice I just sort of slumped awkwardly down and lay sprawling in the ragwort. You know you never notice how knobbly a flower is until you're lying in it.

Once down I smiled in as lazy a fashion as I could manage: "This place is really rather romantic, don't you think?" There was a blade of grass poking me in the ear.

"Romantic?"

"Oh, yes," It's amazing how prickly grass can be, when it puts its mind to it; "Just imagine if this were a scene from a novel."

He frowned doubtfully. Or at least the lower half of his face did. I think. It was a little hard to tell from where I was lying.

And the grass really was very prickly.

Something crawled over my ankle.

"With the sunshine, and the flowers and everything," I waved a hand dreamily at the nearest thistle, and tried to look as though I was contemplating the loveliness of the scene around us, instead of frantically wondering *was that a bee or a wasp?*

He frowned harder. At least I thought he did. I had never considered it before, but lying helplessly in a secluded field with a relative stranger could put one at a slight disadvantage. *And it was crawling up my leg.* I propped myself up on my elbows and took a better look at him. Yes, definitely frowning. "You don't think so Sir? I mean Norman, no, dear, um, Norman dear?"

He shook his head, "It's just..." he gestured at the scene with slightly more vigour than I had used, dislodging the bluebottle from my foot as he did so; "I don't think I've ever read a novel with a picnic in" He reached a hand into the basket as he added; "*or* strawberries."

"Well," I said, "Somebody's bound to write one sooner or later. They can't just keep putting heroines into gothic castles and blasted heaths: they'll run out of room!"

He laughed: "I don't think they set the things in real castles. They make them up to suit the narrative"

"What? So they just say to themselves "I think I'll put a castle in this" and then make the place up out of thin air?" I considered this news. I didn't think I liked it. "So if someone was writing a book about an island, say, they could just invent one, even though there are plenty of perfectly good islands right here?"

"Ah, but they wouldn't be the right *kind* of islands. They'd need the sort of place that sends a frisson of fear running down your spine. The sort of place where horrors lurk around every corner, and shades flit mournfully from the shadows. No one could feel suitably imperilled here, for example: it's simply not horrible enough."

I contemplated our surroundings, the rest of the morning's exhibits, my own unfortunate attempts at haunting, and the way everyone *still* went silent whenever he entered a room, and wondered exactly what he would consider "horrible enough".

I supposed burning to death might almost be sufficient.

It was just as well I'd given up on the idea of frightening Norman away: the man was clearly too unflappable to live.

More to the point he apparently read romantic novels.

I don't know why that surprised me. I knew for a fact that he'd had books in his house when I was there, but somehow I'd assumed they were all weighty histories, or books of theological conundrums, not thrilling adventures like The Mysteries Of Udolpho, or The Mad Monk.

This posed a problem: most of my seductive ploys had been culled directly from the pages of various novels. I hadn't had a great many to begin with, most novelists preferring to draw a polite veil over the actual mechanics of the seduction, so that by the time I had discarded such non-starters as Be A Wealthy And Beautiful Widow, or Serve His Mother Faithfully Until She Dies Of Old Age, I had been left with barely a handful of alternatives. Still, they had been something.

Now, regretfully, I abandoned them. I consoled myself with the thought that they probably wouldn't have worked. And it wasn't as if I even owned an umbrella, anyway.

But now what was I supposed to do?

Could I possibly perform a seduction extempore? I didn't much like my chances.

I wondered what Molly would do? Probably something incredibly straightforward and effective, I decided, but I had no idea what.

Just be yourself insisted the Molly in my mind.

Well that was a terrible idea.

It was, however, the only idea I had.

I pasted on my most convincing smile, drew a shaky breath, and prepared to romance the Reverend as myself. Whoever that was.

"I suppose it makes things easier," I ventured, dragging my attention back to the subject at hand; "with all those oubliettes and hidden stairways to keep track of. And you can always add a secret passageway, any time you need a daring escape."

Norman nodded "Or a really impenetrable dungeon, if you need your heroine to languish for a while."

"And then," I warmed to my subject; "when you want the hero to rescue her, you just add a long forgotten tunnel, or a hidden door and let him come upon it entirely by accident"

"Or he can win over the laundress," suggested Norman; "and convince her to bring him the key."

"Oh no," I corrected; "not if the *heroine's* locked up. Beautiful laundresses only yield to the hero's blandishments if *he's* the one in gaol."

"I don't know why they do it either," I added, thoughtfully. "I mean, you'd think if someone was in service with a wicked baron or what-have-you, then they'd have to be used to dealing with tragic heroes locked up in the dungeons. It seems silly to abandon a well paid job just because some half-baked protagonist bats his eyelashes at you. And why is the Baron worrying about the state of his prisoner's small clothes anyway?"

"I suspect" Norman answered, laughing, "that the laundress is there largely for the sake of her basket. She has to smuggle the poor man out of his durance vile in something, after all"

I scowled at this: no wonder my seduction had been going so badly. How was anyone supposed to properly plan their romance if the writers kept just making things up as they went along? I felt a sudden deep animosity toward authors everywhere. It was as if they *wanted* me to fail.

"But why should she suddenly decide to help him anyway?" I argued; "Here she is, a hardened reprobate who has probably seen dozens of pretty idiots end their days at the hands of the wicked whoever-it-is, but one glance at our hero and her heart apparently softens. What makes him so special?"

"I imagine," said Norman; "that it's some special quality of heroes. We never see the other poor souls after all: they could be anyone and as far as the author is concerned they don't really count, but *he* is tall, dark, handsome, a matchless wit, a peerless swordsman, possessed of every imaginable skill, charming to women and yet always faithful to his one true..."

"And that's another thing!" I interrupted this litany; "Why is the hero so impossibly perfect? You could never actually meet anyone like that. You couldn't fit that many virtues into one human being if you tried. They'd probably explode.

And if you did meet one," I added; "They'd be the most annoying creature imaginable. Swanning about being perfect at everyone. I mean, honestly, did you ever see such a person?"

I looked up, expecting Norman's eyes to dance with the same laughter I'd seen there a moment ago, but instead he sighed and looked a little sad.

"I have, in fact."

"You can't have!"

"No, really," he insisted; "My man, Cecil: he's tall and handsome and dark and witty and good with his hands and...all of those things" he tailed off, wistfully.

I could see his point: it must be awfully depressing to feel constantly overshadowed by his valet. And Norman wasn't the sort of person to fire someone for being competent and attractive. Besides, what could he put in the reference? *"Cecil is neat, well mannered and performs all tasks to the highest standard. Reason for dismissal: Cecil is neat, well mannered and performs all tasks to the highest standard."* It seemed a touch unlikely.

Still, he couldn't possibly be as perfect as that. To begin with his name was "Cecil". Nobody romantic was ever named Cecil. Or Norman, for that matter.

I decided not to mention this last, but: "He can't possibly be as perfect as that."

"No, he is" and Norman sighed again, more hopelessly than ever.

"Well tall, dark and handsome isn't to everyone's taste" I consoled hastily; "Some people prefer blondes after all. Besides, I'd rather share my life with a good conversationalist than a dashing blade"

"Yes," he sighed; "that's what Cecil always says."

"I'm sure you'll like him," he added, shaking off the megrim with an obvious effort; "he should be here by tomorrow evening, you know, and I'm looking forward to introducing you. I'm sure you'll get along famously."

He had put a brave face on things, but it was clear that talking about the handsome valet had put a pall over our cheerful conversation. It was time, I decided, for a change of scenery, and perhaps a change of plan.

"It's almost sunset," I said, pulling myself to my feet and dusting off the crumbs; "Come on, let me show you that cove".

14

It was not almost sunset.

Even the lateness of our start, the size of our tour and the ineffectual clamberings of the tourists in question had not quite conspired to make us take luncheon at dinner-time.

Still, I thought, glancing up to where the sun tilted towards the horizon, that hardly counted as a lie: the sunset wasn't so very far off now, and in fact by the time we had reached the cove it would *very nearly be* almost sunset. Almost.

Accordingly we set off at a neat pace, skirting past the Sentinel Stone with entirely reasonable haste and pushing through the long grass back to the path. Once there it was an easy walk, down past the unholy well, over a thoroughly secular bridge, and we found ourselves on the road past the cliff where...The cliff where...It was the cliff...

Look, it was the cliff where they held the sacrifices, alright? The cliff long hallowed by fumes of sacred smoke, the cliff where the God would come to feast, the cliff where Lord Whatsisname of the Worcester Golds had set his muslin frock on fire.

The cliff where even now stone faced men and stern faced women would be constructing a bonfire.

I swallowed, looked away, and tried to think about something else.

Thinking about something else would have been a lot easier without Norman Poltwhistle. Not only because he was lolloping along in such cheerful unconsciousness that he may as well have worn a sign around his neck reading "Helpless Innocent", but because he wanted to climb the ruddy thing.

"It's not safe," I argued with awful veracity.

"Oh but look," he pointed toward the path; "there's a sort of natural track up this way, I don't think it would be difficult at all."

"You can never tell with cliffs," also true; "the stone could crumble away under your feet."

Well it could. It wasn't likely, but it could.

He squinted upwards: "I think there are people up there."

"I don't see anyone." I glared stubbornly at the cliff-face.

"No look, up there." He cradled my face in a way that would, in other circumstances, have sparked victorious rejoicings, and tipped my head up toward the cliff top.

I screwed up my eyes against the sun: "No, I don't see anything. And besides," I added in a burst of inspiration; "if there were anyone up there they'd probably want to be left alone. We wouldn't want to interrupt them, would we?"

This seemed to do the trick, for Norman ceased protesting and continued down the road, repeating "Ah." and "I see." at intervals, and keeping his eyes so firmly fixed in the opposite direction that I wondered exactly what he thought he did see.

After that I had a little trouble thinking of anything to talk about, for some reason, so we carried on in mostly companionable silence until we came to the stretch of sand-and-pebble beach that led to the cove.

At this Norman burst into a surprised exclamation: "But I've been here!"

He turned to me, alight with excitement: "Could this be where the boat tied up, the night I came here?"

"Very probably," I said; "It's the best place for it, for the water's calm over here, and most of the fishermen stick to the deep water on the other side of the Island"

"But then," he paused eagerly; "does this mean that any other visitors would be likely to arrive here too?"

"Certainly," I said, then added hastily; "But they couldn't see into the cove from here: that would be completely hidden."

I needn't have bothered: "But this is wonderful!" he turned in a slow circle, taking in the rough beach, the weathered mooring post, and the steep stone wall behind us; "It couldn't be better!"

I didn't quite understand his enthusiasm for identifying local landmarks, but I supposed a gentleman must have his hobbies; "Now, where's this cove you mentioned?"

I took him to the cove, where we spent some minutes staring out at the sea and pretending that the sun was a lot lower in the sky than it really was, before we gave up and decided to explore the inside instead.

Inside was mostly water.

"It's not usually like this" I insisted at his crestfallen expression; "it must have been a very high tide or something."

The front half of the cove was entirely filled with a deep pool of sparkling, cold water, and the feathery weed that covered the surrounding rocks was not dry and springy, as I had expected to find it, but soft, green, and verdant.

On the whole the scene did not lend itself to seduction. Not unless one was a mermaid anyway. Or a siren perhaps. But I had a terrible singing voice.

"Look!" I announced desperately: "It's quite dry further back," well I hoped it was; "and these rocks are wonderfully soft." and slippery, I noted, hastily adjusting my balance on the one I had climbed onto; "Why don't we go a little further in?"

He looked supremely unconvinced by my pretended optimism, but we edged our way past the pool anyway and crept carefully over the slick, weed-covered rocks to the back.

Inside was not much more inspiring.

For just a moment the cool air was wonderful: the faintest stirring of breeze like the gentlest of kisses after the cloudless heat outside. After that it was just chilly and uncomfortable. I looked around the gritty, grey interior, scrabbling frantically for something to say.

Fortunately Norman was happy enough to speak for both us.

He poked into every crack and corner, exclaiming over the quality of the light, the rock formations, the slimy green weeds on the slimy green rocks, while I nodded encouragingly, and did my best to look attractively nymph-like.

At first he seemed quite unmoved by my undine charms, preferring to rattle off questions about this rocky shelf, or that odd-shaped stone. I was just casting a dubious eye over the slime-coated stones around the pool, wondering whether the effect of reclining by the edge and trailing a negligent hand in the admittedly opaline waters below would be worth the inevitable muddy green stains, when he suddenly broke off his litany of questions - *"And you say we'd be completely hidden from anyone outside?"*- placed a gentle hand upon my shoulder, and murmured "Ladybird."

Well, it wasn't the most romantic pet-name in the world but at this stage I'd take it.

I turned to him, breath catching, a sudden blush painting my cheeks. This was it: this was what I'd been working for and now it was happening and I still didn't know whether I was more afraid to fail or to succeed.

"Norman?" I breathed.

He lifted his hand: "She must have got blown off course, poor thing." And he held up the bright, little, crimson beetle for my inspection.

Well honestly! What sort of a man lures an innocent impressionable young woman into a secluded cave then, when she's hidden away from any hope of rescue, and tremulously awaiting her shameful deflowering, shoves an insect in her face? Norman *bloody* Poltwhistle, that's who.

He turned away, oblivious to my outrage, and walked off, presumably to release his captive to the world outside.

I watched him go, fuming in indignation, wracking my brains for a suitable response.

"Get back here and ravish me properly" probably wouldn't strike quite the right note.

For want of anything constructive to *say* I decided to try posing a little more obviously instead. The spotless nymph act clearly wasn't having the desired effect, so I abandoned the artless-trailing-fingers-through-the-water idea in favour of showing off my ample if uncertain charms to the best advantage.

I shuffled carefully over the rocks until I was standing on the tallest, overlooking the pool. Once there, I untied my carefully Molly-dishevelled hair and allowed it to float in a soft cloud about my face and shoulders. I shifted my weight onto one foot, turning the other daintily inward and giving a suggestive tilt to my hips. Finally I assumed my most serene expression and leant forward, allowing the glimmering light from the pool to dance over my rapturous face and Poet-vaunted abundance.

I felt like an idiot. I held the pose and tried to envision myself as Aphrodite.

"There she goes!" My would-be amour, having launched his beetle, ambled back into view.

I posed harder, angling my shoulders back and leaning forward to lift my chest.

"Poor little mite: just imagine if she'd been here when the tide came in!"

I schooled my face into blissful serenity and waited for him to be overwhelmed by my beauty. I was incomparable, I told myself firmly; I was a captivating siren; an irresistible enchantress; a goddess beyond all... I slipped off the rock and landed in the pool.

The water hit me like a blow to the stomach, knocking the air from my lungs and leaving me breathless. Even after the cool of the cove it was freezing.

My skirts ballooned wildly before my eyes, blocking out my vision, then rapidly darkened and sank beneath the surface. I stood, up to my chest in the icy brine, my stockings, shift and stays all soaked, and drew a great, gasping, shuddering breath.

God of the Island it was cold!

At the edge of the pool, Norman blinked at me owlishly: "Did you mean to do that?"

I abandoned my first three answers in favour of shivering uncontrollably, then, once I had regained control of both my voice and my temper, managed an acceptably polite "No! N-no I did n-not!"

"Well don't you think you'd better get out then?"

Of course I did, but it was easier said than done.

Even wading through the pool was a challenge: the weight of the water dragging down my woollen skirts to wrap like a hobble around my calves and knees. I staggered towards the rocks, half walking, half swimming, clawing a path for myself with my arms as my feet tottered helplessly along the bottom. Once there I drew myself upright with the excessive dignity of a drunkard and considered my predicament.

I couldn't get out. Waterlogged clothing is, as I may have mentioned once or twice before, quite unbelievably heavy. In the laundry, given a long enough dolly and a firm place to stand, I could just about manage it. Here, with the weight of waterlogged wool compounded by the weight of waterlogged me, and with no helpful lever in sight, I could not.

I hauled futilely against the rocks, hands sliding as the weed and slick stone sliced against my palms.

Norman looked at me for a moment, his head on one side, then took off his greatcoat. Was he planning to ravish me *now?*

It seemed not. Coat folded neatly to one side, he carefully rolled up his sleeves and came to crouch on the rocks opposite me.

"Here," he held out a hand; "Can you reach me?" I reached; "I think if you hold on and sort of push against the side with your feet, I may be able to pull you out."

I had the sudden irresistible image of myself overbalancing and landing him in the pool beside me. Would we ever get out? Would we be stuck here till the water finally filtered away and our clothes dried enough to release us? Would anybody think to look for us here? Would we - and here was a thought - be trapped in this cove until after the bonfire?

Alas for this brilliant last: I had, while I was thinking, been pushing off against the stones and now, instead of toppling to his temporary doom, Norman gave a great tug and heaved me neatly up and out of the water.

Freed from the pool, I shot forward at a quite unseemly rate and landed, flopping like a fish, on the shingle floor.

I grabbed hold of the wall and staggered to my feet. Somehow, now that I was out of the water I felt even colder than I had while I was in it.

Norman wiped a wet tendril of hair out of my eyes.

"My poor dear" he murmured; "you're like a block of ice."

Warm me up then I thought, but even if I'd been able to keep my teeth from chattering I don't think I could have made myself say it.

He rubbed at my chilly hands: "I think the best thing to do would be to get out of those cold, wet clothes," *oh, but maybe;* "and into my coat" *Or maybe not;* "It's warm, and thick, and it should do to keep you covered until we get back to the inn."

He paused for a moment, thinking: "It isn't that far, really, is it? If we go straight there and don't stop to look at the scenery, I mean."

I considered pretending that it was, in fact, that far: far too far for me to walk on my poor chilled toes, with the ground so rough and my good boots wet through and useless.

Alas, dear sir, I fear you will have to carry me. No, it was pointless. Even if he agreed to it he would probably drop me. Or put his back out, rendering himself incapable of either disqualification *or* running away.

Worse yet, he might carry me all the way there, and deposit me tenderly down in the main room of the Inn, in front of everyone. I should never hear the end of that. And then of course, nor would he, because he would be burned to death.

No, that was a plan that would lead nowhere.

Besides, he'd probably just lend me his own boots. I eyed his feet distrustfully: they'd probably fit, too. No, better stick to the truth. It hadn't done so very badly back in the grove, after all. And also I still wasn't entirely sure that I could actually manage to speak.

Shivering I shook my head, and moved my hands to my laces.

He immediately turned his back. Because *naturally* he was going to be a gentleman about it. I'd have been touched, if I weren't so desperately wishing that he wasn't.

My fingers shook and fumbled as I tried to unpick the damp straggling strings that confined my bodice. I tugged and pulled at the lacing, but to no avail: I couldn't do it. The water had swollen and compacted my tidy bow into a solid lump. I might eventually, in the comfort of my room, be able to peel the knot apart, but now, my numb fingers struggling futilely against the salt-soaked cord, I hadn't a hope. I would have to ask for help.

Shamefacedly I turned to Norman and was met, of course, with his polite, frock-coated back. I drew breath to ask for assistance, then at once clamped my mouth shut to keep my teeth from chattering like a skeleton in a nightmare. Slowly, I breathed in and out, willing the tension in my jaw to ease. "C-c-cold!" I stammered, then pressed my lips together as another bout of chattering overtook me.

"Oh, of course," he turned cautiously and took in my predicament; "let me help you.

He moved to stand behind me, hands going to my waist, clever fingers working at the tangled skein. I felt his breath warm on the back of my neck.

"It's no use," he stepped abruptly away from me, towards his greatcoat; "I'm afraid they'll have to be cut." He fumbled in a pocket for a moment, then approached again, something glittering in his hand. For a moment I tensed nervously as he came up behind me. There might be nobody on Earth quite as unintimidating as the Reverend Norman Poltwhistle, but all the same here I was, in a secluded spot with a strange man, a man moreover whom I had known for only a handful of days, standing behind me with a knife in his hand. It occurred to me that perhaps I had not been clever about this.

There was a tiny *snick* and the tension at my ribs gave way.

"There you go", he gave my arm a friendly pat, "I'll just get the ones in your, um, ah, I'll just see to the rest of these and then I'll leave you to it, shall I?"

I nodded shamefacedly, feeling like an idiot.

But you never *did* know, after all.

Behind me, the cut strings of my best bodice slithered free. His breath tickled the back of my neck once more as he lifted my hair up and over one shoulder, pushing my bodice away down my arms. His fingers made tiny spots of heat along my back. The last fastening of my stay laces gave way.

Now, I told myself, turn round now. Even if he *can* resist a semi-naked woman throwing herself at him he'll probably kiss you back just to spare you more embarrassment. But the moment passed and he let me go.

"Right," I could *hear* him shuffle awkwardly; "I'll just be over, ah, over, over there" and he scuttled off, to the mouth of the cove, keeping his back very firmly turned away.

I draggled out of my wet clothes, wincing at the scrape of salt against damp flesh, wrung out my wet hair, and pulled on the greatcoat. It was ridiculously long, covering me from the neck down and trailing across the shingle like one of Himself's more impractical ceremonial gowns. Still, it was something. Even with it on I was cold down to my bones, but it cut down the chill from the air and would, at least, allow me to walk back to the Inn with my dignity partially intact. I piled Molly's blanket over the top of it, and stuffed my wet clothes into the empty picnic basket.

There. I was safe, mostly dry, and unfortunately decent. Time to head back and try to think of another plan.

I made my way around the rocks, holding up the greatcoat like a medieval lady holding up her gown, and stepped out into the light.

Oh.

It was beautiful.

The sunset, which I had so rashly promised and failed to provide, had arrived at last. The sky was filled with clouds of pink and amber, their edges gold against the darkening blue. Further down the sun blazed in an aureole of dying light, a golden path burning across the sea to end almost at our feet. It was all impossibly lovely.

As I stopped, Norman half turned beside me and lifted the basket from my arm. His larger hand stole into mine, fingers warm against my chilly palm. We stood there, rapt in silent wonder, and watched till the last glimmers of honey gold had sunk into the glossy darkness of the sea.

So we had to walk home in the dark.

You'd think, wouldn't you, that one of us might have reasoned this out beforehand? You watch the sunset, the sun goes down, there's no more sun. Darkness, therefore, should seem inevitable.

It was apparent, however, that neither one of us had thought it through.

We scrambled back over the shore to the road, stubbing our toes on hidden rocks and occasionally tripping into small holes. Through it all, Norman seemed uncommonly cheerful for a man who had managed to walk into the same mooring post three times in different directions.

"I've never seen anything so charming!" he remarked, side-stepping a dip in the path that had absolutely not been there when we came this way before; "and utterly secluded too! Really Dora I never expected anything so perfect."

I wondered whether he could be feigning cheerfulness in an attempt to keep my frozen spirits up, but I decided against it. He wasn't that good a liar.

Even with the greatcoat and the blanket, and with Norman's kindly hand warming mine, I still couldn't seem to keep from shivering, and I was just wondering, hazily, whether I could ask him into my room for a hot toddy *to keep out the chill, Norman dear,* and what might be achieved with a gambit like that, when I noticed a light on the road ahead.

Just at the point where the path leads up to the cliff top.

15

There were probably dozens of reasons the light could have been there.

Someone hunting for a lost sheep, say, or a lost child; someone creeping off for a more successful assignation than ours; a fisherman heading out for the night, my Gammer collecting herbs by the non-existent moonlight. Dozens of innocent reasons, but I knew it was none of them.

Someone had seen us go down to the cove. Someone was watching to make sure we came back again.

Had they spotted us by chance? Had Norman drawn their attention with all his pointing and waving at the cliff top? Or had they been watching all along? Watching him, their precious, spotless sacrifice, or watching me?

Did they know what I'd been doing? Did they know what I'd been *trying to do*?

Perhaps I reasoned desperately, they saw us heading to the coast and wanted to make sure I wasn't smuggling him off to the mainland somehow.

But no, that was ridiculous. If they'd thought that they'd have turned up in a mob and overpowered us by force. There would have been ropes, and flaming torches, and at least one of us would have been knocked unconscious. Someone would probably have made a speech.

The word "inevitable" would have been used.

They wouldn't have left a single watcher, with a perfectly practical lamp.

This was something else.

This was Netta Stanley.

Whatever she had been plotting, whatever schemes had been laid that night under the tree, whatever she intended, for good or ill, it was all about to be revealed.

But was it to be a confrontation or a rescue, an alliance or a betrayal? I ran through the possibilities in my mind, temples throbbing with the effort of thought, discarding each almost as soon as it arose: nothing quite fitted. Nothing made sense.

I shivered. My head ached abominably. I didn't want this, didn't want to stand and face whatever new revelations lay behind that single, baleful light. I wanted to turn back. Wanted to haul Norman away, away from the path and the cliff and the lantern and the latest bloody twist in the miserable tale. But my feet kept moving forward, keeping pace with the pounding in my head with heavy jarring steps, stumbling on the sharp, uneven rocks and sending pain lancing up my spine to rattle my skull even further.

The last rational thought I had was that there *was* no reason for anyone to be there, Netta or otherwise, and that the ominous spot of light must be just another symptom of my by now all-encompassing headache, when we drew level with them at last and the lantern's glow illuminated not Netta, not even Himself, out for a little light gloating, but the self-satisfied face of Mrs Barker.

No, I haven't mentioned her before, you needn't go back and check.

The reason I hadn't mentioned her sooner is that, well, she wasn't really relevant till now.

If this were a more traditionally romantic novel then she'd be sure to have come up by now: watching silently in the church, perhaps, or making kindly yet somehow disturbing small-talk in the Inn. This, however, is not that kind of book, and I had been far too busy trying to save a man's life to run about the Island building a narrative. Besides, I don't really like to think about her.

Mrs Barker was the human embodiment of the word "tut". She was a small, narrow-faced woman, with mousy hair and the complacent attitude of one who never expected anyone around her to amount to much and was very vocally too polite to say "I told you so." She even smiled disapprovingly.

She was the Island's self-appointed guardian of moral fortitude. At any time of day or night she might be found, prying into hedgerows or over walls, twitching aside coverings and prodding haystacks, in the hope of discovering some illicit activity. Not out of mere prurience, you understand. Oh no, the God forfend! No, she was propelled on this quest by her sense of virtue. Other people's virtue, that is.

Out of the goodness of her heart she sallied forth to save us from ourselves and hopefully save someone for the yearly bonfire. Thus far she had been unsuccessful.

Love, as the Poet liked to quote, laughs at locksmiths. It certainly struck two fingers up at Mrs Barker.

Still, she hounded the Island's youth to distraction, made unexpected and unwelcome "friendly visits" to anyone even thinking about courting, and grew every year more frustrated and more driven. She treated me in particular with the deepest suspicion. It was as though the very fact that I could never be found doing anything out of line had her convinced that I *must* be up to something. Or else she guessed at what else I hadn't done, and hated me on principle as one who had got away with it.

She had three colourless children who were not permitted to mingle, were not allowed anything so controversial as an opinion, and were, in general, prohibited from doing just about anything other than saying "Yes, Mother" in the sort of unison that ought to have been creepy but which, in practice, was just horribly depressing. Somehow none of them was ever put forward as a sacrifice.

In short, she was terrifying.

Which is why I think it was perfectly understandable when, cold and wet, my legs scraped raw with salt water, mind reeling desperately with the effort of thought, I saw her glowing face loom out of the darkness, and the first thing that burst from my lips was:

"Nothing happened!"

I know.

Yes, I know.

It was completely unforgivable.

Here I was, on the way back from a secluded hideaway, walking hand in hand with a gentleman, with only his greatcoat to hide my nakedness. The implications were obvious.

I had only to blush a little, stammer awkwardly, and rush him away before he had a chance to spoil things. The story would have been all over the Island by breakfast and even if Norman did manage to untangle it in the end, the time for the sacrifice would have been and gone and he would have been safe for another year.

Instead, I took one look at that sourly smiling face, opened my mouth, and ruined everything. Oh insatiable God what had I done?

I drew breath to take it back and froze on the spot. What could I say? What would convince her now? Now as Norman put a comforting arm around my shoulders and began to explain everything. Now as her lips parted and complacent assurances dripped out. Now with the blood rushing in my ears, blocking out sound and thought, as she lifted the light, as Norman turned me kindly to the road, as she guided us condescendingly back to the Inn.

I don't know how I managed the walk back.

I couldn't think, couldn't speak, couldn't do anything but nod, tremblingly, and go where I was turned.

I don't remember getting back to the Inn.

I don't remember passing through the tap room, or the whoops and catcalls from the early patrons.

I don't remember clambering up the twisting stairs, or changing my dress, or how Norman got his coat back.

I remember Molly looking concerned, and Tom, at one point, pressing a cup of something hot and potent into my nerveless hands.

But perhaps I only dreamed that.

I remember standing at the bar, I remember pouring drinks and handing them around, but to whom or what they said I have no idea. I remember the unreality of it all, and the uncertainty, and the way the room seemed to slip and shift like the tides.

And then it was over, the last patron had gone, and I was in the room I shared with Molly, with a fire in the hearth and a blanket tucked around my shoulders, and everything was still and quiet again.

And I had ruined everything.

My thoughts seemed slow and thick like treacle, but through the slurry of confusion one thing pierced, sharp and clear: Norman Poltwhistle was going to die.

None of it had worked: not the hauntings, not the seduction, none of it.

Probably nothing would have worked, no matter what I'd tried: he was doomed the moment he set foot on our benighted, bloodthirsty shore.

I felt suddenly sick to my stomach, the room oppressively hot even as I shivered under the blanket.

There had to be something I could do, something that would work, something I hadn't tried.

But there isn't, said the slow, sly voice of my inner thoughts, *you've tried it all and nothing works. You've failed him, Dora.*

I tried to push the thought away, grasping for something, some forgotten wisp of hope, something he'd said, a last idea, anything.

There wasn't anything.

The room reeled around me again and I bit down hard on my lip to fight the rushing wave of nausea. From the next room I heard the quiet sounds of someone pottering comfortably about. Norman was getting ready for bed. In a few minutes he would be asleep, and then it would be morning, and he would come down, bright and happy and ready for the day.

And they would take him, and tie him up, and burn him on a pyre, and he would never laugh, or say "Um", or spill his beer, or rescue another ladybird, ever ever again.

A terrible sob lurched from my throat.

In the next room, the movement stopped abruptly.

He'd heard me. I froze stupidly on the spot, pressing the heel of my hand against my mouth to hold back the floods of grief that threatened to overwhelm me.

Was he listening? Was he watching me, his eye pressed tight to the peephole over Molly's bed?

Surely I could do something with this.

Why couldn't I *think*?

He hadn't wanted me in the laundry room, but I could hardly blame him for that.

He'd never even seen me in the bath tub, but after my earlier performance in the tide-pool I had no faith at all that that would have worked.

The closest we had come to anything had been in the strange, sunlit grove, joking over the strawberries and talking about books. But even then something had been in the way, something had stopped him taking that last step, had stopped me, if I was honest, from asking "Do you want..."

Well he didn't want, it seemed, and nor did I, but still something had got to be done.

We were friends, that was the worst of it.

He wasn't just some random visitor I had tried and failed to save. I liked him, liked the way he believed in the best in people, the way he tried not to laugh when someone said something appalling, the way that laughter burst out sometimes, unbidden, as though I'd tricked it out of him, and his ridiculous look of outrage when it did.

I didn't want to sleep with him, I would never want that, but I didn't want to carry on in a world without him in it.

So why couldn't I think of something?

Books...

That was the only thing we had in common, really: books, and ridiculous stories, and an interest in lost, curious, forgotten things. But what could I do with that?

I could stand here, reciting love poems, and he'd just think I liked the sound of them, and he'd turn around, satisfied that I was perfectly well, and go to bed and in the morning...No.

I could tap on his door, perhaps, and murmur: "Did you know, Norman, that tonight is May Eve, and they do say that if you go out into the fields and..."

No. He'd find it all fascinating, no doubt, but he wouldn't want to try it for himself.

Or, I acknowledged glumly, not with *me*.

Besides, he was a vicar, turning away from pagan temptations was more or less his job.

It occurred to me, not for the first time, that my compatriots had chosen depressingly well.

Blast them.

No, don't blast them.

Don't waste time.

Think of something.

Pagan temptations.

What about them? My mother's old books wavered tantalisingly before my eyes. Crabbed old texts written by crabbed old men, telling improbable tales of dark deeds, midnight revels, and charms spun out in the new moon's light.

"New moon's light" my elbow. It was a new moon now, that was why there wasn't any light: because there wasn't any ruddy moon.

It was a new moon now…

Pages of fevered imaginings, horrible deeds and the tortures that had to be wreaked before anyone would confess to them. Stories of old women turning into hares, blighting crops, dancing naked under the blackened sky to ensnare the hearts of…Ensnare the hearts of…

It was bloody stupid.

But it was the only idea I had.

Hardly daring to move, I stood and listened. No movement. He must still be at the spyhole.

Cautiously, heart thundering, I undid my laces and stepped out of my clothes.

What now?

Was I supposed to chant something?

Were there words?

Were there *steps*?

I took a cautious hop and a step and listened out again for movement.

All quiet.

I skipped a couple of steps, wincing as my flesh bounced and rippled with the movement, and clapped a hand across my bosom to stop it flailing painfully up and down.

Words. I needed words to dance to.

I drew a breath, span dramatically about, pointed one toe, opened my mouth and

"If I had a donkey wot would not go,"

What? No! Not that!

Too late: I had made my choice and I would have to stick to it.

I twirled neatly around the space, declaiming as I did so: "D'ye think I'd wallop him? No, oh no! But gentle means I'd try, d'ye see?" I hopped back and forth, tossing my hair and barely keeping out of the fireplace; "Because I hate all cru-el-tee.

If all -had been -like me -in fact," I threw back my aching head, arching my back, and almost careening into the foot of Molly's bed; "There'd be no occasion for-" I stopped, catching my breath, as my ears caught the sound drifting in from the next room.

A soft sound, gentle even, but unmistakable.

A soft, gentle, damning snore.

I sat down on the floor, in the heap of my discarded garments, and sobbed.

16

I'm not sure how long I sat there.

Long enough that my eyes were red and my throat was raw.

Long enough for the fire to burn down and my skin to pebble over with the cold.

Long enough that I was still sitting there, choking on little, silent sobs, when Molly came in and found me.

Perhaps she opened the door and immediately rushed to my side. Perhaps she was struck dumb by the sight of me, and stood, not knowing what to do for long uncertain minutes.

Either way, the first I knew of her presence was when a crisp white shift dropped neatly onto my head, a warm arm fell around my shoulders, and her soft voice murmured "Oh Dora, whatever happened?"

I sniffled into the nightgown for a while, wiping my eyes on its enveloping folds and trying to discover some semblance of dignity. Then I realised that I was sitting naked on the bedroom floor crying into a nightie and that at this point dignity was so far beyond me as to belong to a different era entirely.

Possibly the Pleistocene.

I wiped my face on the nightdress and told her the whole sorry tale.

The whole tale didn't take very long, even taking into account all the times I had to stop and muffle a fresh bout of tears in the nightie. After the third such interruption, Molly tugged the dress away from my face, turned me around, and let me sob into her shoulder instead.

I'm not sure why that helped, but it did

"...and I've tried everything," I howled incoherently into her collarbone; "I dressed up like a ghost, and I stared at him, and I did his laundry and bathed and dragged him all over the Island, and I danced like an absolute idiot but nothing's *worked!*"

If Molly found anything unconventional in my attempts at a wooing she had the tact not to mention it.

"And tomorrow," I broke off for another paragraph of weeping; "tomorrow they're going to kill him and there's nothing I can do!"

Molly heaved the kind of sigh that probably got her admirers very excited indeed: "There's always something you can do," I snuffled a little in refutation but she held firm; "It might not be easy, or even particularly helpful, but there's always something. Now, start at the beginning." She pulled back to look me in watery, swollen eyes: "What did he say when you told him?"

I looked away, unsure of what to say.

"You did tell him, Dora, didn't you?"

Well of course I didn't. The words died on my lips. I had been so certain that he wouldn't believe me. No sensible person would, surely, when faced with something so outrageous. It had seemed the most certain way imaginable to losing his confidence altogether. Now, in the face of Molly's straightforward question, I was suddenly a lot less sure.

Molly read the unspoken no in my face and groaned.

"*Dora,*" affection and exasperation mingled in her voice; "how in the world were you supposed to save him if he didn't know he needed saving?"

I had heard many stupid things in my life. From my Gammer's insistence that aconite was good for the croup, to pretty much anything ever uttered by Himself With The Orchard, my life had been bounded with stupid things.

Nothing in my life, though, had ever sounded quite so stupid as the words "I thought I could seduce him." coming from my own two lips. Molly clearly agreed. She stared at me as though I had said I could fly us both to Jupiter. And perhaps take in a little luncheon on Saturn while I was at it.

"You thought you could...you, Dora Makepeace, thought you could..." she trailed off, clearly dumbfounded at the very idea.

I would have been insulted if she hadn't been so very, very right.

There was another exquisite sigh.

"Well how did you ask him, then?"

"Ask him?" My voice sounded very quiet, or perhaps it was just a very long way away.

"You know, did you say: "How's about a roll in the hay your reverence?" or ask him to help pull your garters up, or what? How did you ask him?"

"I didn't," if anything my voice had grown even smaller and quieter; "I thought I could just, you know, hint at it."

"Hint at it."

"Yes."

"Like, "Oh woe is me, here I am trapped on this lonely isle with only seven dozen lusty specimens to choose from, if only some kindly Vicar would come sweep me off my feet and into his bed." That sort of hint?"

I thought the sarcasm was a little uncalled for.

"No," I sat up straighter, adjusting the nightdress; "I made opportunities, and hung around looking available and, you know, I *hinted* at it."

The sigh this time would not only send any number of ardent admirers into joyful raptures, but spread happiness to the hearts of any hitherto disinterested swains as well. Unfortunately the only person there to see it was me. "You can't just hint at people!"

"You... can't?"

"Course you can't! How're they meant to know what you're hinting *at*? How're they meant to know there's anything to *be* hinted at? You can't just stand around acting cryptic and expect everyone to just somehow *understand* you"

"Not everyone," I pointed out; "just him. I was trying to be subtle."

"But that's worse!"

"It is?"

"Well of course it is! How was he supposed to pick up on your blessed hints if they're too subtle to notice!"

I wilted slightly: "I just thought he'd understand"

She sighed again, but it wasn't remotely tantalising. "You always do that: either you expect people to understand things, and then you're disappointed when they don't, or you just assume everyone's an idiot, and you're all surprised at them having the slightest bit of sense. Some day you're going to have to make your mind up whether everyone's secretly some kind of fiendish genius, or whether we're all so dim we'd have to look up at the clouds to see if it was raining.

"Well which is it then?"

"It's both. Everybody's both." She looked at me oddly; "Even you're both. Maybe 'specially you."

I wanted to argue, somehow, to say that of course I didn't think like that, or that almost everyone on this Island really was an idiot, actually, or that it wasn't my fault if Norman Poltwhistle couldn't follow the perfectly simple directions that I'd neglected to actually give him, but what came out was: "Well I never see you warning anybody!"

"Course you don't," retorted Molly, simply; "That's cos I do it sneakily, behind everybody's backs."

"You know," she added, with the hint of a smile; "*subtly.*"

"Like who?!"

"Like Netta Stanley for one."

I gaped at her: "Netta Stanley wasn't eligible! Everyone knows she came here to escape a cruel marriage."

"She did," Molly nodded agreeably, "Only she escaped it before it happened"

"Then how did she know-"

"Oh it def'nitely *would have been* cruel. If she'd gone through with it. What with her not being interested in men and all".

I was dumbfounded: "Are you sure?"

"Very sure." Molly grinned: "Strictly ladies-only is Netta," the grin widened; "I've *checked*." "You have?" I sat up properly, woes temporarily forgotten in the face of this unexpected news, "You mean you've asked her or - "

"I mean I've *checked*." The grin was definitely lascivious-looking now; "Extensively. Checked again the other night, too."

But…the other night? Which night? Last night? The night before? Had I been tying myself in knots over nothing more dreadful than Molly's admittedly awful love-life? I tried to formulate some kind of rational enquiry, but all that came out was: "*And?*"

She blushed shyly.

Shyness was not something I'd ever associated with Molly before. It rather suited her.

"Oh, Dora," she whispered, hushed, as if afraid to speak the words out loud; "I really think she might be, you know, *it*."

"Really?" Netta was nothing like Molly's usual swains. She wasn't loud or brash or swaggering in the least. She was quietish, plainish, hard working and, I suspected, kind. Come to think of it, she was probably exactly what Molly needed.

And with that thought, the last of my confused indignation disappeared.

"Is she good to you?"

"Very."

"And she makes you happy?"

She nodded vigorously.

"Then that's alright then." I threw my arms around her, nightdress abandoned in my lap, and hugged her gladly; "If anyone around here is going to find their happy ending I'm glad it's you, Moll. You deserve it."

"Well so do you." She jumped up, suddenly determined, and started rifling through her chest throwing things out onto the floor.

"Here's what you're going to do: you're going to put on that nightie," she paused, considering the crumpled, tearstained mass of linen; "a different nightie, and throw this over the top," she tossed me a very familiar black, hooded cloak; "and you're going to go into that man's room and you're going to tell him everything."

"But he'll think I've run mad!"

"Maybe he will, maybe he won't. You can't know until you try. If he believes you, you take this candle," a hefty brass candle holder landed at my feet; "and you make a run for the fishing sheds. You know those things are never locked properly." I did not know this, and said so; "Well they aren't, so you should be able to find a boat. Get in, grab an oar each, and row like fire for the mainland. I'll pack up your things and send them after you later."

She made it all sound ridiculously simple.

So naturally I had to argue. "But what if he doesn't believe me?"

"Then hit him over the head with the candlestick and *drag* him there."

I hesitated: "You know, knocking people out isn't as easy as you'd think. Blows to the head are notoriously risky."

"So's being thrown on a bonfire, Dora: *go!*"

I scrambled into my shift and picked up the cloak. It was rich, black velvet, deep and soft, embroidered at the neck with seed pearls. It must have been the last piece of finery Netta had left. And she'd given it to Molly.

"I can't wear this!"

"Course you can! The ties go in the front and the hood goes over your head. Even you can't mess that up." She tied it for me anyway, and thrust the candlestick into my hand. This time I got as far as the doorway before I faltered.

"But what if..."

"Look, at some point you just have to have a little faith. In him, or yourself, or just in good luck, you've got to trust something. Otherwise you'll never do anything at all."

And with these words she put her hand to my back, shoved me firmly out into the corridor, and shut the door behind me.

Out on the landing I raised my candlestick bravely aloft and gave a decisive rap on Norman's door.

He didn't answer.

I rapped again, a little less certainly this time.

A delicate snore drifted through the wall.

I knocked again, rather more quietly, then more quietly again, then stopped with the foolish realisation that I was knocking to get Norman's attention, but trying to do so very gently *so I wouldn't wake him up.*

Since this was clearly ridiculous I stopped knocking and considered my options.

I could knock louder, and hope the noise would eventually bring him to the door, if only to ask me to go away. This was probably the most practical plan and if I had had any faith in my ability to penetrate Norman's slumbers I would have embraced it wholeheartedly. Knowing however that he had managed to fall asleep while I was careening about the next room like a baby elephant with a turn for moralising verse, I rather doubted my merely hammering on his door would do anything to disturb him.

I could walk boldly into the room and shake him awake. This, I felt, was what Molly expected from me: bold, assertive action leading to a definite result. It was simple, it was sensible, it was straightforward. It was a thoroughly practical choice. It was also the only choice, unless I wanted to stand shilly-shallying on the landing all night.

Of course, shilly-shallying could have its advantages. The longer I did it, the longer I wouldn't have to explain myself to Norman Poltwhistle, for one thing.

In fact, if I did it for much longer the whole decision would be taken out of my hands altogether and I'd never have to explain anything at all. This, of course, would be because he would be being slow-roasted on the cliff top, but after all one couldn't have everything. I shook myself firmly: No, shilly-shallying wouldn't help me: decisive action it was.

And before I could argue myself out of it again, I seized hold of the door handle, flung open the door and marched into the room prepared to drag Norman out of his slumber by main force.

He was awake, which put something of a crimp in that plan.

I managed, having half-reached out to shake him before I noticed, to restrain myself enough that I didn't actually throttle the poor man, set the candlestick down on the nearby table and said weakly "You're awake."

"I am, yes, I mean...sorry?" he sat up and blinked himself into wakefulness. "I never can stay asleep when there's someone outside my door, somehow. Is, is everything quite alright?"

"No." I sat down on the end of the bed and looked forlornly at the floorboards; "Everything's all wrong."

"Oh dear. Really? Is there, um, anything I can do?" His kind eyes spoke of nothing but the earnest desire to help me in whatever way he could, hopefully quickly, so he could get back to sleep.

I disappointed him."You could start," I observed, "by putting on your trousers."

"My trousers?" I wasn't sure whether his discomfiture sprang from being asked to change his clothes in front of me, or from the realisation that he was going to be required to get out of bed; "I'm really not sure that's quite..."
I was ruthless."Your trousers, please, Sir." I said, because a gentleman's bedroom in the middle of the night is exactly the place to take refuge in formality, and I'll tell you everything."

And I turned to face the wall, to give him some privacy and not incidentally so I wouldn't have to look him in the face.

The bedsprings creaked as he got up and started puttering about the room.

I fixed my eyes firmly on the lime washed wall before me and began: "What would you say, Sir, if I told you that everyone on the Island was plotting to kill you?"

There was a long silence.

"Tomorrow morning," I added, by way of filling the gap; "in a slow and exquisitely painful fashion."

The silence persisted a while before he replied in a rather quiet, thoughtful sort of voice: "I don't know: is that something you're likely to tell me?"

I took a deep breath.

"Yes."

"You're quite sure?"

"Yes."

"And this isn't something you could be mistaken on at all? Some fevered hallucination resulting from hypothermia perhaps?"

"*No, Sir.*"

172

"Oh dear. Really?"

"I'm afraid so Sir."

"Well you'd better tell me all about it then. You can turn round by the way: the trousers are, ah, firmly in place."

I turned, albeit reluctantly. He had on, along with the trousers, his greatcoat, his round-lensed spectacles, a pair of sturdy-looking boots, and an expression of deep concern, such as one might assume on receiving some terrible news. Or, of course, if one suspected the person they were talking to had gone completely round the twist.

I faced my doom: "Sir, everyone on the Island is plotting to kill you, tomorrow morning."

"Slowly and painfully. Yes, you said. Have you any idea why?"

"Oh yes."

"Well do you think you could explain it to me?"

I sighed: this was not going to be easy.

"Could you imagine," I began, cautiously; "an island where the people still worshipped a long forgotten god, ancient and terrible, and where, at the turning of the seasons every year, they offered up a single virgin sacrifice to the God's sacred fire, to ensure a good harvest and prosperity for all?"

I paused awkwardly: "Weather and virgins permitting," I added.

"I suppose I could imagine something like that," he conceded.

"And could you imagine Sir, Norman I mean, could you imagine that on that Island virgins might get a little bit hard to come by, after a while?"

"I imagine that might be the case, yes," he said.

"Then imagine," I continued, as impressively as I could manage, given the panic I was in; "the people of the island waiting for some poor unfortunate traveller to arrive in time for the bonfire. Only the travellers don't come, out when they do come they're no use, so the islanders get more and more desperate and in the end they give up and..."

"Convert to Christianity?" he suggested, hopefully.

"No sir."

"I didn't think so," he admitted.

"No sir, Norman, sir, what they do is, *they send out to the mainland for a victim.*"

"They...do?"

"They do. They send a couple of fellows off to the mainland to ask whether they can spare us a Vicar, only it's an awful thing, we haven't had one to minister to us for years, getting downright heathen we are, terrible it is, terrible.

Oh, they add, but better not make it a family man: the Rectory's in such a state. No, a nice, quiet bachelor will do just perfectly. And maybe they play up the charms of the local ladies just a bit, to help catch the nice quiet bachelor's attention.

And, Norman, when they do what do they find but a nice helpful Bishop, terribly happy to oblige, knows just the fellow, never been any sort of a hand with the ladies but an awfully good man and terribly devout. And he packs the man off the next morning.

Can you imagine that?"

"Oddly enough," his voice was rather shaken; "I can."

"Well then," I arrived at the crescendo; "imagine no more Sir, Norman I mean, for that island is..."

"It's this one isn't it?"

"Is the very isle we stand...yes, it is, how did you know?"

"It was sort of obvious after a while," he gave an apologetic little smile; "and the Bishop is my uncle. It was a very good impression. Have you met him?"

I was nonplussed: "...no?"

"Oh, well you sounded exactly like him. It's just the sort of thing he'd do, too: send me off to some miserable - sorry - some picturesque little island to make a man of me, and get me horribly murdered by cultists in the process." I wanted to point out that we were a religion, not a cult, but somehow this didn't seem quite the time. "Well so much for his brilliant scheme: the local women are hardly going to want to have their way with me if everybody's plotting to kill me. When you say everybody, do you mean absolutely everybody, by the way, or was that a spot of decorative hyperbole"

"I mean everybody!" I paused; "Except me. And Tom and Molly quite like you. And there's a lot of people that don't really care what happens, but they won't do anything to stop it."

He slumped dejectedly. "I thought my Sunday service went over rather well."

"Oh it did. Everyone really enjoyed it, it's just they'd enjoy setting you on fire even more".

"Setting me on fire?"

"Yes, and then the crops will grow, and fish will fill the nets, and we might get some better weather for a change, but not really because it doesn't work"

"Doesn't it?"

"No."

"Then why do they do it?"

"Well it's better than doing nothing, I suppose. This way at least it *feels* like they're achieving something, even if it is only going to make things worse in the long run," when someone finally wonders what became of you I carefully didn't say. "Besides, the bonfire's nice and it brings the whole community together. There's usually a bran tub for the little ones too."

Exactly what was *in* said bran tub I thought it better not to mention.

He looked a little queasy as it was.

"And you've come to rescue me."

"That's right."

"You couldn't have done something a little sooner?"

I was stung: "Well what do you think I've been trying to do?"

He blinked at me: "I have absolutely no idea: what have you been trying to do?"

"I've been trying," I almost yelled; "to seduce you"

To say that he looked taken aback was to lose the perfect opportunity to use the word flabbergasted.

"You... have?"

Yes!"

"*When?*"

"All ruddy week!"

"Oh." He looked thoughtful for a moment: "I'm terribly sorry: I didn't notice."

There was a long, uncomfortable pause, broken only when, in a rather wobbly voice he managed to ask: "*Why* were you trying to seduce me?"

"To disqualify you."

He looked, if anything, blanker than ever.

"So you couldn't be a virgin sacrifice any more."

"Oh, I see," he shifted a little; "That's rather amusing actually because you see technically I'm not... wait a moment. How on Earth were you planning to achieve that? Were you going to set the scene with candles and rose petals, woo me with poetry, turn my head with compliments, then, when I was as putty in your hands, murmur sweetly "Breeches off love: I need to save you from a slow and agonising death"?"

Half of me wanted to recoil at his crudeness, while the other half wanted to ask whether the thing with the poetry and roses would actually have worked.

In the end I wished I'd done either of those things, because what I did was say: "No, I wasn't going to mention it."
I hadn't realised that he'd been avoiding my gaze until he stopped. "You weren't going to mention it?"

"Well no, I mean, it didn't seem that important really, I mean, don't men just...I mean, I didn't think it mattered *why* just as long as we um..."

When attempting to remove the foot from one's mouth, it is vitally important not to wedge the other one in there too.

"I was trying to save your life, you know"

"Yes, I know."

There is a kind of stare that doesn't seem much at first, but the longer it goes on the more uncomfortable its target becomes, until finally one feels about as small, insignificant and unwelcome as a particularly repellent and biting gnat. I had not previously imagined Norman Poltwhistle to be capable of such a look.

It seemed the night was full of revelations.

"Dora, I know you meant well, but to entrap someone into intercourse under false pretences is," he shook his head sadly; "well, is rather awful, actually"

As it happened right now I *felt* awful. And ashamed. I wanted to say so. Or mention the whole "saving his life" thing again. Or at least ask how managed to use the word "intercourse" like that without sniggering. Only somehow I couldn't find the words. Or look him in the eye. Or do anything much but stand, wishing I was anywhere in the world but there.

After what seemed like a thousand unrelenting aeons he took pity on me: "Well, least said soonest mended," he shook himself, like a dog coming in from the rain; "You didn't actually do anything so very terrible, in the end, and I suspect if it had come to the point you might very well have found you couldn't go through with it after all."

I thought about all the times I hadn't gone through with it and elected to say nothing.

"Now, did you have some sort of escape plan in mind, or are you just here to, ah, herald my demise?"

I took this for the olive branch it was: "I have a plan sir."

"Oh, good. What is it?"

"We escape."

"That's…it?"

"Pretty much. We leave the Inn, sneak down to the fishing sheds, steal a boat and head for the mainland"

"Oh. That sounds very sensible and straightforward."

"Thank you," I decided not to mention that it was Molly's plan.

"Can you, ah, sail a boat?"

"Not yet, but I've heard it's best to learn by doing."

Now was not the time to point out that his choice was between possible death at the hands of an inexpert sailor, or certain death on the annual barbecue.

"But we don't really have to sail very far, Sir."

I'd thought about this while prevaricating on the landing. You see! Shilly-shallying has its uses! "We just need to get far enough out that they can't get us in again in time for the sacrifice. Then either we drift innocently back in to shore and you arrange a proper return trip in your own time, or we drift all the way across to the mainland and you head back to your own little parish"

"And if we drift out to sea instead?"

"Then we'll probably be eaten by mermaids, which will be something to tell the grandchildren about, at least."

"I see," he looked rather grim for a moment, then squared his shoulders resolutely and began throwing his things higgledy piggledy into his bag.

"No time for that!" I caught his arm, almost taking a block of shaving soap to the face in the process; "They'll come looking for you at dawn, and we can't be far off now."

We couldn't: Molly rarely got to bed before, as she liked to put it "The evening's started getting light again," and even allowing that she'd come home early out of concern for me, she still wouldn't have got in until some hours past midnight. And then I'd wasted another hour or so sobbing into her shoulder and at least that long again confessing the whole sorry tale to Norman. Even as I spoke the sky was doing its pedantic best to disprove the claim that it is always darkest before dawn. It was past time to go.

"Here!" I brushed aside his reluctance and snatched up a sheet of paper to scribble a note:

Molly

Fleeing for our lives

Please send luggage to

I looked at him enquiringly until he took the pen and scribbled something illegible and ink-spotted that might possibly have been an address.

Love to you and Tom,

I thought for a minute before adding *and Netta* then signed my name with a flourish.

How's that for decisive action?

"Now come on!"

For a wonder, and for the first and only time in this narrative, he came.

We tiptoed down the stairs, which was ridiculous for there were only Tom and Molly to hear us, and out into the Inn yard.

As the chill night air caressed my skin I basked, for a single ridiculous moment, in the knowledge that I, Dora the barmaid, was escaping by candlelight under cover of darkness, in my nightgown and flowing velvet cloak, with my long hair streaming - well, frizzing - in the wind.

Even the knowledge that I would eventually have to deal with the stains - probably tarry and immovable - on said garments could not quash the frisson of delight at finding myself so perfectly a heroine of romance.

And then the bastard cock came squawking out of the darkness and pecked me on the foot again.

I did not cry out.

I didn't so much as squeal.

I didn't even give a single startled gasp and faint swooningly into Norman's arms, which I feel in the circumstances would have been an entirely appropriate and heroine-like course of action.

I merely pushed past the cockerel and continued on my way with poise and dignity.

So the ruddy bird went for the other foot. And stayed there, flapping and clucking like an idiot, making it impossible to pass.

"Go away" I hissed, frantically; "It's not dawn yet you silly bird. Molly'll bring your breakfast when it's good and ready."

Norman watched this exchange with interest.

Well it wasn't his toes that had just been assaulted.
"Perhaps he's trying to tell you something?"

"No he isn't," I untied my cloak and flapped it fruitlessly at the cock, trying to chase him off; "He's just a useless great lump who can't tell the time and doesn't want to wait till breakfast."

With a final lunge I dropped the cloak over the frantic fowl, bundled him up, and heaved the whole lot over the wall into the poultry yard, offering a silent apology to Molly as I did so.

"There, that's done it. Come on," and we carried on across the yard.

Just as we got to the gate I turned back, struck by a sudden thought.

"Hold on. What did you mean when you said you weren't technically..."

And that's when someone hit me on the head.

17

My first thought was that I owed the cockerel an apology.

Well, no, my first thought was *Ow*, followed by the traditional *Where am I?* but as the reality of our predicament sank in it occurred to me that I might perhaps have been a little swift to rush to judgement.

It occurred also that I soon might not be able to apologise to anyone, ever again.

Driven by this realisation I twisted round to look for Norman. "Norman," I hissed.

"Whuh?" he blinked himself into consciousness and looked painfully around us.

"Norman I'm really sorry. For the whole trying to save your life thing. Without telling you I mean. Because I completely understand that motivation changes things, and proper consent is *so* important, and you deserved to know..."

"Dora!" he winced slightly at the sound of his voice; "Is this really the time?"

I shrugged as best I could in the circumstances: "I might not get another chance."

"Ah," he acknowledged the truth of this; "Yes, well, least said soonest mended perhaps. I accept your apology. You meant well, after all, and it's not as if you ever actually got anywhere. Who knows? Perhaps you would have been more successful if you *had* told me why you were doing it."

Well. It was nice to know that one's embraces might not actually constitute a fate worse than death.

That was all rather moot now, though, as from the look of things death was now very firmly on the cards for both of us.

We were tied, side by side to a large wooden stake that had been thrust into the middle of a vast pile of green boughs, driftwood, and scraps of kindling. Our hands and arms were bound up past the elbows, and our feet too, and some idiot had stuck wreaths of flowers on our heads. Norman looked pretty good in his, to tell the truth.

A little way off from our perilous throne stood a crowd of Islanders, all bearing lit torches and looks of cheerful anticipation.

This struck me as terribly unfair.

If this were being written properly we would have come to our senses in some gloomy prison or other, without the audience, and - I gave one hand a surreptitious tug - with rather less secure bonds. What, might I ask, was the point of having a handy landmark like the fishing sheds, looming so tall, dark and foreboding in my imagination, if we *weren't* going to end up imprisoned there with but a single candle stub to lighten the gloom and, incidentally, help us burn through our bonds and escape in a handily available boat?

Instead of which, here we were in the middle of the action and with more than half of the usual ceremonial having apparently happened *off the page*. It all seemed very badly plotted indeed.

I dimly recognised that I might be complaining about the wrong thing, but my head hurt worse than ever, and since there didn't seem to be any readily available way out of this, and my attempts at subtly undoing our bonds were getting precisely nowhere I felt I might as well settle down and enjoy my sulk.

Now that I took the time to look - well, glower - around, I realised that the assembled throng was somewhat smaller than usual.

Oh, Himself With All The Dead Ruddy Trees was there in - oh dear - a puce satin robe and "symbolic" mask, waving a dramatic arm and declaiming portentously, and Old Man Morris was sitting on a stool, commenting on something or other with a slightly confused look on his face; but now I really *looked*, it seemed as though quite a lot of the usual luminaries, the people you would generally expect to see handing out drinks, cracking jokes, or accosting the other attendees with books of raffle tickets, were nowhere to be seen.

Nor was the bran tub, nor the hoop-la, nor - and I flinched a little at the thought - the hog roast.

And there weren't any children there at all.

This was vaguely comforting, really: if nothing else it seemed as though most of my compatriots had concluded that, when push came to shove, they didn't actually want to be responsible for burning anybody to death, even if they hadn't actually had the courage to stop it.

And I wouldn't be featuring in any nightmares for the little ones.

On the other hand, well, they hadn't done anything to stop it, either. And their absence meant there wasn't much chance of appealing to anybody's better nature to get us out.

I wasn't sure most of this lot even had better natures.

I could see a large assortment of the wooden faced, wooden headed true believers, who would cheerfully burn - sorry *who would burn* their own aged grandmother if once they'd decided it was the right thing to do.

Then there were several truly desperate, dirt-poor farmers who were ready to clutch at any straw, even an unfortunately human-shaped one, if it meant they might just make it to next year's harvest. It hardly seemed fair to blame them for trying to stay alive. But I was tied to a pyre and about to be burned to death, so I ignored fairness and hated them for it anyway.

There were quite a few landowners of the kind who seemed to have difficulty recognising other, less fortunate people as people even when they weren't on top of a sacrificial bonfire.

There was the Lord of the Fruit Flies' crowd of crack-brained acolytes, all far too caught up in the Ancient, Mystical Ceremonial of it all to bother noticing that their spiritual experience entailed the agonising death of two real, tangible human beings.

There was - there always was - one idiot with a penny whistle, who was liable, if he didn't shut up soon, to find himself joining us among the flames.

And there was Mrs Barker.

She in particular seemed to be positively rejoicing in our imminent doom.

She waved her torch in a particularly emphatic manner, nodding her head at all Himself's most ridiculous pronouncements, and shooting me some positively spiteful looks whenever everybody's attention was elsewhere.

I told you she had it in for me.

Eventually her religious fervour reached some sort of crescendo and, flailing her torch so vigorously that she looked set to ignite her fellow officiants before she ever came near to the bonfire, she began to throw in a few pronouncements of her own.

The wind stole most of their words before I could catch them, but I managed to make out Himself's darkly intoned "One who would come here of his own free will."

Well that's hardly fair, I thought, *after all the trouble you went to bring him here.*

Before I could work up much indignation on this point, however, Mrs Barker waved her torch again and chimed in: "One who would come here a virgin!"

Well that was the whole point of the...hold on a moment!

And feeling very relieved that the genius with the ropes - *still* not untied, thank you so very much - hadn't added a gag as well I raised my voice and shouted back: "Oh no he isn't!"

"Not technically," I added, into the spreading silence.

"Go on," I hissed, flapping my barely loosened hand frantically in his direction; "Tell them."

"Oh," said Norman.

And: "Um."

And: "Ah, well, when you, um consider all the aspects and, ah, variations of, um, of human courtship then I think it fair to say that..."

And then he stopped, looked quite exquisitely uncomfortable, blushed as red as any of the Poet's metaphors, and added: "And why's Dora here anyway? She's clearly not a virgin"

I just about bit back the words *"I'm not?"* and settled for staring at him in confusion.

"Well obviously," he added, shifting slightly under my gaze; "Just look at her..."

He paused for a moment, squinting at me like a particularly seductive chicken; "Eyes?" he hazarded.

My stare became just the tiniest bit flinty.

"Hair then," he amended; "Or her..." he pulled the face of one who desperately wants to wave his hand in a vague yet expressive circle, but who is constrained from doing so by several feet of best hempen rope.

"Abundance," I suggested.

"Yes, that, um, what?

Anyway," he rushed on; "she's clearly a very attractive girl who must have any number of suitors, and certainly can't be, um,"

"Qualified," I muttered under my breath.

"Yes, um, certainly can't be qualified to be your sacrifice. So why is she up here?"

One of the stone faced men stepped forward. I vaguely remembered him as a shepherd who would occasionally step into the Inn for a drink before going back out to do whatever it is that shepherds do. He was always perfectly polite and respectful, as I recalled; perhaps a little shy, but happy to stand his round and helpful with the empties when I came to clear the tables. A pleasure to serve in fact.

There was nothing very pleasing about him now. "She's here," he sneered; "to pay for her crimes. She tried to stop the sacrifice: she can burn with you."

"Indeed" intoned the Master Of All Vaguely Apple-Related Nicknames; "So is it written. So it must be. "

And at that point I lost my temper.

"Where?" I demanded.

They all looked at me blankly.

"Where is it written?" I wanted to shake a finger at him, but settled for nodding fiercely in his general direction; "Because I've read everything there is to read on this ruddy island, and had to bring more than half of it here myself, and in everything I've read there wasn't one word about tying people up and bunging them on bonfires. There's no rule written anywhere that says if you try to disqualify someone from sacrifice you end up sacrificed yourself: you're just making it up.

In fact there's nothing written down about any of this: we just do it this way because that's what our great-grandparents did, or so they say, and they did it because their grandparents did, and so on and so on and ruddy so on, and at no point did any of them stop and bother to ask themselves whether any of it worked."

I took a breath to try to calm myself down, then realised there wasn't any *reason* to calm down and forged on: "Because of course it doesn't work! You can't just fix the weather! You can't get good crops from bad soil, or make fish swim against the tide, or grow bloody apple trees on a cliff by the bloody sea!

None of it's any *good*, and it isn't going to change because a bunch of idiots got dressed up in a lot of funny robes and set fire to a man whose only crime was being too bloody good-natured to know a lot of murderous gits when he saw them. Um, Sorry Norman."

He shrugged as best he could: "No no, I quite agree, do carry on."

I carried on.

"And you know it won't work. You do, really. You aren't utter idiots. Not all of you. You know the ground here's no good for farming, and the weather's too miserable, and the fish won't come no matter what you do. You just don't want to face it.

Because if you look at it all, really look at it, and think for a minute, then you'll see that there isn't an easy answer to any of this. Things really are that bad, and there's no simple choice you can make that will stop them being that bad. And that feels completely hopeless.

So instead of looking any further you get scared, and you look away, and you look for any other answer you can find, however stupid.

And you tell yourselves that this will work, that against all logic and reason and natural philosophy, you'll be able to make the sun shine brighter, and the earth become fruitful and the ruddy little fishes swim the freezing bloody sea, by sacrificing a good man to a God none of us have ever even seen.

Because action feels better than inaction, and at least this way you can pretend you tried.And you'll tell yourselves things are getting better, won't you?

All year round you'll scrape what living you can get from the soil, and you'll herd your poor starving sheep over the hills, and pull up a few putrid, bony fish, and look for imaginary blossom on dead trees, and you'll tell yourselves it's better than last year: "These things take time," "Wait and see," "It could be worse."

And then a year'll go by, or two, and it will *be* worse, and of course you won't admit you're wrong so you'll go looking for something else to blame: "It was the wind from the north," maybe, or "All the fish got stolen by them from the mainland," or "This wasn't the bonfire that I voted for."

And when you've run out of scapegoats you still won't be able to admit it didn't work, because then everything that'll have gone wrong since might be your fault."

"And if it didn't work," I added, as an afterthought; "If you admitted to yourselves for a moment that this really didn't work, then you'd have to admit that what you're doing now doesn't serve any high-minded ideal or greater purpose at all. It's not special. It's just murder. And I don't think you want be murderers. So why don't you untie us, and pull down the stupid bonfire, and we'll do what we can together to make the best of the awful ruddy world that we're stuck with."

I looked at them appealingly.

Nobody moved.

Of course they didn't.

Every word that I said had been true, especially the bits about not wanting to accept it.

And also, I realised with a foggy sort of dread, I had just called them all idiots several times over. People tend to take offence at that sort of thing.

"But he isn't even a virgin!" I wailed.

There was a stirring in the crowd: a murmuring, soft and slow but surely building, like a shift in the stars, a ray of hope breaking through the clouds of our despair, and then...

"I bet he is." Came a voice from the back.

"Well he isn't." I retorted.

"Prove it!" Came another voice. There was a general murmur of assent.

"For goodness' sakes, Norman, tell them!" I begged.

He gulped.

"Well, um. If it comes to that. The thing is..."

He turned several shades paler and coughed rather helplessly as though trying to clear his throat: "The fact of the matter is,"

He took a deep breath and with the face of one facing the gallows, and thus rather better off than we were about to be if he didn't get a move on, declared in a small, defiant voice: "I've been sleeping with my valet since we were nineteen years old."

There was utter silence.

"We met at the university," he added; "He was the most beautiful man I'd ever seen. And I love him quite desperately."

And the silly man looked as though he was about to faint.

I gaped at him.

This was what he'd made such a fuss about? This was what he'd been so afraid, even on pain of death, to say?

I mean, it explained a lot.

It explained everything.

It certainly made me feel a lot better about my own shortcomings in the seduction market.

But why make such a fuss about it?

Here he was, about to expire horribly for the crime of never having indulged in carnal affections and instead of clearing his good name he ummed and ah-ed and looked as though he were going to be sick.

In his place I'd have cheerfully declared that I'd been riding that man into the coverlet twice a night and three times on Saturdays.

For some reason this course of action didn't seem to have appealed to him.

I looked at him in annoyance, wishing not for the first, or even the third time, that I could get a hand free to gesticulate with: "Then why didn't you say so?"

He looked uncomfortable.

"Well, you know."

I didn't know, and said so.

His discomfort deepened: "Well, it's just that, if it got out, well, my name would be quite ruined, and his too, and my Uncle would be furious, and then there are the legal repercussions, though I'm not quite sure what those would be, but I'd certainly lose my living and…"

He tailed off: "People would disapprove," he ended, simply.

This was news to me. Still: "Would they," I asked in an admirable impersonation of a calm and rational individual; "tie you up and throw you on a fire and burn you to death?"

"With me alongside you," I added, by way of an afterthought.

"Well, no," he admitted, avoiding my gaze; "hang us, maybe, or perhaps that's just for the Navy, I'm not quite sure, but it would all be terribly unpleasant whatever happened."

I gaped at him. "But that's barbaric!"

He gave me a look that, gentle and unassuming as it was, nevertheless expressed the fact that here we were, about to become so much human crackling thanks to the dubious belief that this would somehow move the Sun and shift the tides in their courses, and did I really want to talk about who had the worse social conventions, right this minute?

He had a point, I suppose, but I did my best to look quietly unimpressed, all the same. "Anyway!" I announced, remembering all at once that we'd had an audience for this exchange; "He's *obviously* disqualified, aren't you, Sir?"

"Oh quite, quite", he agreed, hastily; "Completely ineligible I'm afraid.

A malus interdictus, you might say" and he glanced at Himself with what I would swear was a twinkle in his eye.

"And," he added, gaining confidence as he spoke; "Since Dora has clearly done nothing worse than attempt to forestall a terrible act of gross impiety, I think the best thing would be for you to simply cut us both down and…"

"You're lying!" Snapped Mrs Barker.

"Oh, no, not at all," Norman smiled guilelessly; "it simply isn't the sort of thing one lies about. Or not where I'm from, at least: I realise your customs may be somewhat, ah, different than I'm used to but, really, if you would like to wait a little while, Cecil should be here soon and he can, um, corroborate my story or not, as he sees fit"

"You're trying to postpone the sacrifice"

"I wouldn't dream of it!" he declared, and there was a definite sparkle in his eyes: he had done it, he had got them now, we had *won:* "I promise ma'am that if that man says he doesn't love me then I will cheerfully climb back up here and light the fire myself."

Do you know, I honestly believe he meant it.

I would have said so, too, but at that moment:

"It doesn't count!"

"What do you mean it doesn't..." I began, but she shrieked down upon us with a frenzy in her eyes. "It doesn't count", she snarled; "Intercourse is between one man and one woman. Your shoddy little affair doesn't count!"

This was news to me.

And clearly to everyone else as well.

But before anyone could say "What?" or "Rubbish!" or "Now hold on a moment," she had plunged her torch deep into the heart of the pyre.

It caught at once.

It shouldn't have. Even a small, well built fire generally needs a fair bit of coaxing to get underway, and this one, besides being more than usually on the large side, had been constructed with a mind more more for sense of drama than for ease of lighting. The green boughs which constituted much of its bulk should have resisted the flame for a good while at least.

Unfortunately this seemed to be the point at which life finally decided to start behaving like a romantic novel at last, for the whole lot went up like a shot.

It must have been a magnificent sight: the flaring pyre throwing tongues of fire up into the golden sky. The driftwood in particular gave off a very attractive blue flame. I wasn't really in the best position to appreciate it, unfortunately, what with the smoke, and the heat on my flesh, and the general sense of my own imminent demise. I tried to catch my breath, choked, and tried again with no result. The faces beyond the flames blurred into a vast unseeing mass.

Beside me, Norman was no better off than I.

"Dora," he croaked and broke off to cough uncontrollably; "do you think this counts as martyrdom?" I had no idea and could barely marshal my thoughts anyway, but I tried to say something helpful, choked on the thick, black clouds, and managed to wave one finally unravelled hand in what I hoped was a comforting manner.

So this was it then. My head swam as I drew in lung after lungful of thick, deathly smoke. With luck we'd be unconscious before our flesh began to fry.

I drew a last tarry breath, preparing to utter some deathless last words: "Sic transit Gloria Mundi," perhaps, or; "This is the last time I try to do you any favours," but before I could splutter out even a gasp there was a shift in the silence beyond the flames.

"Personally," came a new voice; "I've always thought virginity was more of a social construct."

"That's what I've always said!" I gasped, then wished I hadn't, and not only because those would make truly awful last words.

The newcomer turned towards me.

He was tall. Taller than any man there, taller than the great pole at the centre of the pyre, taller, I suspected, than any tree. His form was cadaverous, flesh hanging from his stark starved ribs, every joint and bone impossibly defined. His arms were long, claw-tipped and terrible, his antlers seemed to catch and hold the sun. Above his vast, unspeakable maw two eyes, bleak and cavernous, blinked at me mildly.

"What really matters," he confided in a tongue unutterable by man, yet understood by all; "is consent. Did you come willingly to this place of sacrifice?"

"They did! They did!" squawked Mrs Barker; "Accept our sacrifice oh Lord!"

"Oh you rotten liar," I coughed; "You hit us on the head!" I bet she had, too: I could just see her lurking round the corner by the Inn, hoping to catch us in the act of escape.

"Really?" asked the dread lord and avatar of our benighted land;

"Blows to the head can be very dangerous you know."

Fortunately for everyone's sanity, I was prevented from saying "I said that too!" because I was, by this point, about half-way dead of smoke inhalation.

"Still," added the awful, unknowable master of all; "that clearly constitutes duress. I don't see how either of you can be said to have given your consent in this matter." And with that the loathsome, terrible arms reached toward us, that unknowable, blasphemous face blocked out the Sun, and he plucked us neatly from the pyre and set us kindly down upon the grass, a little way from the dumbstruck crowd.

Then, as if as an afterthought he cut through our ropes with one horrible, scythe-like claw.

"This is all very unfortunate," he remarked, sadly; "I suppose the rest of you didn't want to be here either?"

That's where I could have stopped it.

That's the moment that I revisit in my dreams, over and over.

The moment where time flows like treacle and every fibre of my being screams at me to do something and yet all I can do is lie there, helplessly, watching.

That's the point at which Mrs Barker rushed forward, her eyes filled with fervour and piety and thwarted spite.

"We did, Lord!" she howled; "We come here for you!"

"Oh?" remarked the ancient God of the Island, He Who Blesses All Things and Brings The Harvest Home, in slightly more cheerful tones; "Well that's something, anyway." And he snatched her up in one vast thorny hand, lifted her to the immeasurable abyss of his mouth and...

I told you I don't like to think about it.

I watched as he turned upon the crowd, as they began to scream, to plead, to shout improbable, probably made up invocations and, in the case of the more level-headed celebrants to explain that they had changed their minds and since they were very definitely entitled to withdraw consent at any point in the proceedings, they would just be heading off home now, if it's all the same to you.

That last one probably worked.

I hope so anyway.

I can't say for sure because my smoke stung eyes finally filled with tears, blurred and lost all sense of the scene before me; my head, still swimming from the smoke began to ache intolerably once more; and all I was sure of was Norman's hand on my arm and his voice telling me to come on, Dora, come on, now, while nobody's looking.

I wanted to stay.

I wanted to shout "Stop!" or explain that they didn't really mean it, or at least swoon dead away so I wouldn't have to know what was going on.

I wanted, somewhere in my most secret and shameful heart, to ask about the other figures in the circle of carvings, to learn who they were and where they could be found.

I did none of it. I took Norman's hand and, hating myself more than I had ever hated any one or thing in all my life before, I ran, headlong, down the cliff path and away.

Well, ran, anyway. We hadn't got more than about half a yard down the path before we crashed into someone coming the other way and I sat down with a bump.

For a moment I was entirely concerned with stopping myself from sliding the rest of the way on my rear, and with shaking the fog from my eyes so that I could at least see what I was floundering into, but as the world righted itself once more around me I looked blearily up to hear Norman say, a trifle hoarsely perhaps, but in tones of remarkable cheeriness: "Hullo Cecil!"

It was, of course, the valet. Or, as I now understood matters, it was his sweetheart.

Quite probably, going on what little he'd said of the matter, his husband, by Island custom at least.

I blinked away the last of the smuts and prepared to glare at a man who, if he had just arrived a few hours earlier, might have saved so much bother and confusion. And horrible death.

Honestly, I thought confusedly, *if you'd just admitted to existing none of this would ever have happened.*

And then I saw him.

He was exactly as Norman had said.

His hair curled attractively back from a fine brow. His eyes were honey dark and sensitive, yet bore within them a light of mischief. His

lips, by turns sensuous and sensitive, were parted in a quizzical smile. His attire was faultless in its elegant simplicity and he bore himself with such casual confidence and grace that I could easily imagine him fighting off a score of improbably armed foes, from horseback, while at the same time sweeping some hapless swooning ninny off their feet and declaring his affections to the stars.
Probably in verse.

In short, he was quite depressingly like the hero of every romance I had every read. And he was looking at gawkish, fluff-headed, Norman "Budgerigar" Poltwhistle as though he were the most ravishing creature on Earth.

I swear I heard him murmur "Oh, he doth teach the torches to burn bright".

Before I could point out the stunning inappropriateness of that particular statement at that particular moment, however, he gave a dazzling grin and remarked: "Hello Norman, have you been having an adventure?"

At this Norman gave a sort of desperate little sigh and threw himself into his sweetheart's startled arms.

I immediately found myself very interested in the state of my clothes. Fortunately there was a lot of a state to be interested in, and by the time I had catalogued every spot of mud, grass stain, scorch and rope mark, and consoled myself that my hair at least was mostly miraculously unburned, they had largely disentangled themselves and were merely standing, hand in hand, smiling foolishly at each other. Cecil made even that look hopelessly romantic.

As if reminded of my presence by this observation, he looked up at me, coughed a little - whether to get Norman's attention or from second-hand smoke I wasn't sure - and asked casually "Uh, who's your friend?"

"Oh!" Norman shook off his happy daze to wave more-or-less in my direction; "This is Dora, she tried to seduce me in order to rescue me from a lot of murderous islanders, only she wasn't very good at it, and also I'm very, very gay, and quite devoted to you, so we're running away from them instead."

Cecil stared at me: "Really?"

"Really," my reply was punctuated by a long agonised scream from somewhere behind us; "but it's sort of a long story, so do you mind if we carry on escaping while we tell it?" There was another, rather truncated, scream.

"By all means," he swept me a little bow, seized Norman's hand, and set off at a graceful lope down the path.

I scrabbled to my feet and followed after.

The cliff path is steep and narrow, and neither Norman nor I was in the best condition for climbing, so it took us quite a while to reach the rock-strewn sands of the bay.

By that time most of the story had been told and, after a few last remarks about Ancient Gods from Beyond the Time of Man and the importance of being absolutely clear in one's intentions -which, yes, I know, I *said* I was sorry didn't I?- we all slowed to catch our breath, take stock a little, and look back at the cliff-top. Which now seemed to mostly be on fire.

That'll be all the torches I mused pointlessly, *people really ought to consider basic fire-safety when they're immolating other people alive.* Then I stopped musing, because Norman had said something

"I'm sorry, what was that?" I asked, turning my back firmly on the blazing headland.

"I just asked what you were planning to do now," he repeated; "is it too dangerous for you to go back to the Inn, do you think?"

"I'm not sure."

I thought about it: "I suppose anyone sensible enough to escape from that mess ought to have the sense to realise that there's no point taking it out on me.

Then again, people don't always think like that, and even if they did, there are a lot of parents and spouses and siblings and so on who are going to be looking for somebody to blame: I think it might be best to be somewhere else while they're doing that"

"Well that sounds very wise" they smiled at me encouragingly.

"I think," I decided as I spoke; "the best thing might be for you to give me a lift to the mainland. If there's any room in your boat that is."

I looked hopefully at Cecil: "I'm not really dressed for company, but there're always inns in need of staff, and someone'll probably lend me enough to get by, at least till Molly can send my things."

The thought of Molly brought a pang to my heart, but I quashed it mercilessly: I would miss her horribly, and I expected she'd miss me too, but I strongly suspected that if I stayed gone then Netta Stanley might be moved to give up farm work and take over my job, and that would be nice for both of them. And a great saving on bedlinen besides.

For a moment nobody said anything.

Then Norman looked at Cecil, or Cecil looked at Norman, and there was a moment of that silent communication that occurs sometimes between those who know each other very well indeed or, according to novels at least, are very deeply in love.

Or both, perhaps.

Then as the silence was split by yet another heartrending, agonised scream, Cecil turned to me and said: "Come with us."

"To the mainland, you mean?"

"No, come *with* us. It's perfect: you need a job and somewhere to stay and we need..." he shrugged expressively; "Look, we'll say you're the housekeeper. You can even *be* the housekeeper, if you like: we could probably do with one. Either way, everyone will be convinced you're sleeping together, it'll be the most enormous scandal, and Norman's rotten old uncle will be ecstatic."

He batted his eyelashes at me in an annoyingly charming sort of way: "Oh please say you will, Dora, it's the most perfect opportunity we'll ever have and we can't possibly be a worse proposition than a lot of vengeance-fuelled, murderous cultists."

I wanted to point out that the Islanders weren't actually murderers, most of the time, and that "cultist" was almost certainly not the right word for a people whose God quite literally walked among us, but he misunderstood my hesitancy and ploughed on: "Or turning up at some random inn in a torn nightdress with your bosoms all-" the gesture this time was even more expressive and I clutched reflexively for my absent cloak; "You can't possibly imagine that *that* would go well."

Well, no, now he put it that way, I didn't.

I bit my lip. The suggestion was a tempting one, in an odd sort of way, but could I really abandon everyone and everything I'd ever known to live among strange people and strange ways?

There was another scream, rather closer than before, but that wasn't what decided me.

Norman shuffled his feet a little in the shingle and looked at me shyly.

"You don't have to, Dora, please don't think that: we'll gladly take you to the mainland, and I'm sure we can find you a dress and, and so on so you don't have to, um, but, well, if you wanted to, then, ah, we'd very much like it if, that is..."

There are many ways to communicate.

You can speak plainly.

You can avoid the subject, talk around it, and hope to goodness that someone gets the hint.

You can be teasing, or pompous, or stoic, rhetorical, hyperbolic, or smug.

Meaning can be found in a word, in a glance, in a smile, in the petals of a perfect rose left at the perfect moment in the echoes of a perfect night.

It can be lost, or found, or altered, or chosen to suit oneself. It can be expressed in fifty thousand carefully chosen words and yet still be tragically misunderstood, or it can pass between two people in a flash, without a word or a gesture to express what is truly meant.

As with the silent communication between lovers. Or, I realised, the awkward, stammering uncertainty of a new but very dear friend.

"Alright," I said; "I'll come".

And we got in the boat.

18

I sat in the boat and drifted, both literally and figuratively.

I should probably have been frantically second-guessing myself, overthinking, making plans and worrying and wondering what would happen next. That's what I'd been doing all week, after all. But I didn't. I just sat in the boat and let my mind drift on the gentle lapping of the water.

I could have worried about the people I'd left behind: the ones possibly being eaten alive or burning to death on the flaming headland. I *would* worry about them, later, their plans for me and Norman notwithstanding, but right now, what with the lack of sleep, and the smoke inhalation, and my own narrow escape - well, I just didn't seem to have the energy.

I could have been worrying about Tom, who probably wouldn't be happy about losing a barmaid, *or* suddenly gaining one.

I could have wondered if Netta would fit in or not, how they'd cope, what would happen if it turned out she and Molly weren't right for one another after all.

I could have worried about Molly.

But, somehow, I didn't.

Who had decided, I wondered to myself, that I was the practical one and Molly wasn't?

She'd been practical enough last night, and before that too, any time I wasn't there to assume the burden of practicality for her. You probably had to be practical, really, if you looked the way she looked and lived the way we lived. I just hadn't seen it. She'd always been just Molly.

And I'd been Dora the Barmaid: practical, unromantic, a little too well-read, but a capable hand when there was a tray to be carried or a floor to be scrubbed. A bit-part player in other people's lives, there to offer a word of friendly encouragement, or a not *too* witty remark, then dole out the drinks and saunter off, out of the story again.

I'd been Dora the Barmaid so well and for so long that I'd almost forgotten how to be anybody else.

And then I'd stepped outside of my role. I'd tried to change things. And no, in the end I hadn't really changed a thing, and yes, it would probably all have played out pretty much the same without my interference, but maybe that wasn't the important thing after all.

Because *I'd* changed.

I had, as they say, met someone, and everything had changed, not for the rest of the world, but for me.

Because while everyone else had just seen Dora the Barmaid, Norman had seen... Well he'd still seen Dora the Barmaid, but a Dora the barmaid who was a little more Dora and a little less Barmaid.

And I'd seen a friend. Oh it wasn't friendship at first sight: I hadn't even loathed him in an amusingly prickly fashion that would somehow inevitably lead to friendship. But I'd got to know him, a little, and while I might have thought he was a hopeless idiot to begin with, over time I'd realised that. Alright, that he was still a hopeless idiot, but an idiot I quite liked, all the same.

I suspected he might think something similar about me.

So here I was, being swept off my feet like the heroine at the end of a novel.

I might not have the romance, and here I glanced over at the front of the boat where Cecil - handling the sails with predictable competence - and Norman -gazing at him like a myopic pigeon- were playing out their own soppy conclusion, but I'd never wanted that anyway. What I had was a chance, a chance to make a new life, with new friends, in a new land.

And maybe the new land was only a few miles from the old one, but that just meant that I wouldn't have to completely abandon the friends I'd had before. Maybe I'd find I went from Dora the Barmaid straight to Dora the Housekeeper or, if Cecil was right to "Dora the Vicar's slut" but still I'd have the time to decide who that was, to let people see me in a new light, to be the feckless, pretty one; or the one in charge; or not "the" anything at all, but just me.

Maybe the mainland would be completely different from the Island, maybe it would be almost the same. Maybe people were just people, wherever you went.

At least I had a chance to find out.

And with that last thought, I lay back in the boat, with the sun shining full in my face and nothing whatsoever to do, and drifted off into, if not a happy ending, then at least a hopeful beginning.

Printed in Great Britain
by Amazon

82562626R00119